The promise

One day my best friend Kim died.

Before she died, Kim made me promise to contact her.

I didn't want to.

But she made me promise.

So then I tried.
    And tried.
    And tried.
    And tried.
    And tried.

Turns out I suck at talking to dead people.

OTHER BOOKS YOU MAY ENJOY

The End
or
Something Like That

ANN DEE ELLIS

speak
An Imprint of Penguin Group (USA)

SPEAK
Published by the Penguin Group
Penguin Group (USA) LLC
375 Hudson Street
New York, New York 10014

USA * Canada * UK * Ireland * Australia
New Zealand * India * South Africa * China

penguin.com
A Penguin Random House Company

First published in the United States of America by Dial Books,
an imprint of Penguin Group (USA) LLC, 2014
Published by Speak, an imprint of Penguin Group (USA) LLC, 2015

THE LIBRARY OF CONGRESS HAS CATALOGED THE DIAL BOOKS EDITION AS FOLLOWS:
Ellis, Ann Dee.
The end or something like that / by Ann Dee Ellis.
pages cm
Summary: As the first anniversary of her best friend Kim's death nears,
fourteen-year-old Emmy tries to fulfill her promise to make contact with Kim's spirit,
but she gains new perspective from unexpected connections.
ISBN 978-0-8037-3739-6 (hardcover)
[1. Death—Fiction. 2. Best friends—Fiction. 3. Friendship—Fiction.
4. High schools—Fiction. 5. Schools—Fiction. 6. Self-esteem—Fiction.
7. Family life—Nevada—Las Vegas—Fiction. 8. Las Vegas (Nev.)—Fiction.]
I. Title.
PZ7.E4582End 2014 [Fic]—dc23 2013020975

Speak ISBN 978-0-14-242263-2

Printed in the United States of America

1 3 5 7 9 10 8 6 4 2

* * *

*To my Asher, for his sensitive soul and wise thoughts, and
to my mother, who knew better than I did that this is not the end.
And that's a word with a bark on it.*

• 1 •

One day my best friend named Kim died.

• 2 •

Before she died, Kim made me promise to contact her.

• 3 •

I didn't want to.

• 4 •

But she made me promise.

• 5 •

So then I tried.

   And tried.

   And tried.

   And tried.

   And tried.

Turns out I suck at talking to dead people.

• 6 •

Another person who died was my earth science teacher named Ms. Homeyer.

She didn't know my best friend Kim.

I did not like Ms. Homeyer very much.

She died almost a year after Kim died.

Her funeral was one day before the anniversary of my dead best friend's death.

I rode the bus to Ms. Homeyer's funeral.

• 7 •

I wore my mom's fancy turquoise dress with the sequins because the black dress I got for Kim's funeral didn't fit anymore, and I didn't have anything else.

When Skeeter got on the bus, I could see in his face that I'd made the wrong decision. I could see it right when he looked at me.

"Crap," I said.

"What?" He sat next to me.

"Nothing."

"No, what?"

"I look dumb," I said.

He was trying to keep his face normal even though he knew what I was talking about.

"You look good," he said.

"Shut up," I said.

"No. Really. You look pretty."

This made it worse because I did not look pretty. I never look pretty.

Skeeter was in his Little Caesars uniform with his huge headphones around his neck, and I was in a cocktail dress with my huarache sandals.

"Do you really want to do this?" he asked. "We don't have to."

Ms. Homeyer had died on Tuesday, and Skeeter didn't get why I wanted to go to her funeral so bad. I didn't get why I wanted to go so bad either.

"I told you, you didn't have to come," I said.

"I'm here, aren't I?"

We were crammed on the seat because the bus was full: probably a matinee just got out at one of the casinos.

I gripped my bag. This was my first time being down on the strip since Kim died, and I still hated it. So much.

Skeeter and I sat there and people were sweating and I felt sticky and as we drove, Skeeter kept trying to talk to me, but I kept saying, *Skeeter. Stop talking.*

And he'd say, *But did you see the blah blah?*

And I'd say, *Skeeter, don't you want to listen to your stupid music?*

When we turned on Flamingo I watched the people outside and tried to tune out Skeeter's voice.

I heard a lady telling her toddler to pull her panties up. A guy hacking something out of his throat. A kid talking loud in Spanish.

Outside there were things.

Usual things.

Drunks on benches, skanky ladies on cell phones, and tourists taking pictures. Skeeter's voice came back in. His dog and fishing and *Stone Temple Pilots*, and blah blah and we turned the corner onto Paradise, and there was a man holding a sign and dancing.

The sign said,

DR. TED FARNSWORTH IS WATCHING YOU!

COME TO HIS SEMINAR *TALKING BEYOND*.

TO FIND OUT MORE!

SATURDAY, MAY 26TH

AT CIRCUS CIRCUS RESORT!

GO TO TALKTODEADLOVEDONES.COM FOR MORE INFO.

My heart thumped.

DR. TED FARNSWORTH IS WATCHING YOU!

Thumped.

I had been e-mailing Dr. Ted Farnsworth every day for months.

E-mailing. Tweeting. Messaging. I even sent him a post-card.

All I ever got back were form responses.

THANKS FOR YOUR E-MAIL! REMEMBER THE VEIL IS THIN! YOUR LOVED ONES ARE WAITING!

His website said all his shows were postponed until further notice.

But now

He was here.

In town.

The day before Kim's death anniversary, THE MOST IMPORTANT DAY IN YOUR MORTAL AND YOUR BELOVED'S IMMORTAL LIVES, and he was here.

We drove away from the sign.

We drove and drove and drove and drove and drove away from the sign, and I tried to calm down.

I tried to calm down.

Then.

At the corner of Paradise and Sands, I saw her.

At 5:23 on Friday, May 25th, in the middle of Skeeter's sentence I saw the wrong dead person.

I saw Ms. Dead Homeyer.

According to Dr. Ted Farnsworth, if your best friend dies, you can talk to her afterward.

She can call you. You can call her. On special occasions she can come down and hang out with you. And if you're really in tune, she can move into your closet.

Kim circled all the dates she was going to appear after she died.

"I'll do your birthday and my birthday," she said, the pen in her teeth. "Both at Red Rock?"

Kim's favorite place in the whole world was Red Rock Canyon. Mine sort of was too. I wasn't sure.

We'd gone hiking there with her mom, Trish, and my

dad had taken us a couple times, and sometimes Kim would talk about if she got old enough, she'd move out there.

"You'd want to live there?"

"Wouldn't you want to? Like camp every night under the stars?"

I thought about it for a second. "I guess?"

I wasn't much of a camper. I hated bugs.

"We'll both move out there," she said.

"Okay."

So for both our birthdays after she died, we were going to meet in the canyon.

There were some other dates. Her mom's birthday, my mom's birthday. And she kept reminding me, "Don't forget the most important one, don't forget the most important date is the anniversary of the day I die."

"You're not going to die."

"I'm going to die, Emmy."

"You're not."

Then she died.

✳ ✳ ✳

25

So on my birthday, fifty-three days after Kim, after her heart stopped, the first important date, I got everything Kim and I had agreed on.

I got the cupcakes.

I got the Fresca.

I got *Ladyhawke* loaded up on my laptop.

I got three boxes of candy: Snickers, Skittles, and M&M's.

I got her favorite book, *The House on Mango Street.*

And I put on my white cargo pants and a white T-shirt. Dr. Ted Farnsworth advocated light colors for dead-people talking.

Mom said, "Don't you want to do something special for your birthday?"

She stood in the kitchen, watching me as I packed the soda in my backpack.

She'd made Joe go get me doughnuts for breakfast, but now he was at basketball practice and Dad was out golfing.

But Mom.

Mom was waiting for me.

"I have somewhere to go," I told her.

"All day?"

"All day," I said.

She gripped the counter. "Where? Where do you have to go all day long?"

She was trying to be patient with me. Her therapist told her to be patient with me. I heard her tell Dad that, and Dad said, "I think that'd be a good idea, Linda."

And it was a good idea.

I tucked my hair behind my ear and tried to look normal. Like I was her normal daughter on a normal day that was my birthday.

"I'm going to the mall with Gabby," I said.

"Gabby," she said.

"Gabby," I said.

She stared at me.

Then she said it again, "You're going to the mall with Gabby."

It was a bad lie. Mom knew and I knew, that except for the week after Kim died, I hadn't spoken to Gabby for over a month. She also knew that I'd been sitting in my closet every Friday night, and one time I made a doll out of an old sweater. She thought this was disturbing and discussed it at length with my father who told her she was being irrational. I heard them talking through the vent in my closet. It's actually a really good place to hear things.

Mom was quiet.

"Yeah. She wants to buy me some earrings," I said, which was stupid because I don't wear earrings.

I grabbed a box of crackers. I didn't know how long this was going to take and I liked to be prepared.

"Why do you need all that food?" she asked.

I swallowed. "Uh, because we're going to have a picnic afterward."

"A picnic?"

"Yep."

And I smiled.

"Well," she finally said, "okay."

"Okay?"

"Okay."

I opened the fridge and got out some apples.

"You could invite her to go to dinner with us."

"Who?"

"Gabby," she said. "To the Cheesecake Factory."

Dinner. Invite Gabby to dinner.

"I'll see," I said. "But I think she wants to take me out for pizza later."

It sounded so dumb as it came out of my mouth. I was the worst at this.

Then she said, "You don't want to go to dinner?"

Every year we went to the Cheesecake Factory on my birthday. Every single year. This would be the first time we'd be there without Kim.

"No," I said. "It's okay."

Mom stared at me. "Are you sure, Emmy?"

I smiled big and this is what happens when someone knows the other person is lying her face off, and the person lying her face off knows the person knows she's lying her face off, but she keeps lying as hard and as fast as she can because she also knows that the person won't stop her.

Mom wasn't going to stop me.

This was her being patient. She was going to let me do whatever I wanted on my birthday, and she knew it had nothing to do with my old friends.

For the first time since Kim died, I felt love for my mother in her jeggings.

"We might go anyway when you get back," she said, "just for dessert."

I said, "Okay."

And she said, "Okay," and she handed me forty dollars. "Have fun."

"I will," I said.

I walked out the door and got on the bus that stopped near Red Rock Canyon Road.

* * *

The sun was out bright already.

As the bus got closer to the stop, I started to feel nervous.

We'd talked about it so much.

"Do you think I'll be wearing white?" Kim had said.

"I don't know."

She pulled out some grass and started sucking on it. "What if I'm naked?"

"Sick."

"What? It's only natural. That's how we were born."

"Yeah, but you aren't going to appear naked."

She stacked the grass into a pile. "What if all dead people are naked walking around heaven?"

"Ew," I said because I don't like naked people. I once saw my brother in the bathroom and I can't talk about it.

Kim said, "Let's close our eyes and think about it."

I hit her.

"No, really," she said. "Think about my uncle Sid."

Kim's uncle Sid died when we were eight, and I did not want to imagine him like that.

* * *

Now it was my birthday and she was dead and maybe she would show up naked.

I got off the bus and walked up the highway.

It was a long, long walk, and sometimes Kim and I would bring our bikes on the bus and ride to the canyon. But it was hard to ride a bike with all the stuff in my backpack.

So I walked.

A falcon flew overhead. Maybe that was Kim, I thought for a second, but then the falcon disappeared behind a hill. And it was really just a magpie.

After an hour, I got to the trailhead and stopped. Tried to breathe. I was out of shape.

I took a water out of my pack and drank the whole thing. Then I hiked to the rock we'd picked. A flat rock with ruts beat down by the rain.

One Saturday we'd come out to choose the place.

"This will be where I appear again," Kim had said, her arms outstretched, her black hair blowing in the wind. I'd held my breath as she stood there, and then she looked at me and started laughing.

***

Now I was here alone.

Waiting for her.

I took a breath. I can do this. I can do this. I can do this.

I pulled out the quilt with the blue buffalo on it. I set out all the food.

Then I sat down.

The sun was hot and I should have brought a hat.

People walked by.

A guy with a beard asked me what time it was.

I ate a Snickers bar. Two Snickers bars.

Then ten.

Some crackers.

Two apples.

I sat there from nine in the morning until eight at night.

Alone.

• 9 •

I wasn't going to go to Ms. Homeyer's funeral.

I didn't want to go.

She yelled at us for no reason.

She ate tuna fish out of the can at her desk.

She didn't know any of our names.

And one time, on one of my worst days, she asked me, in front of the class, if I'd forgotten to wear deodorant.

Why would I go to her funeral?

I wouldn't.

But for some reason, I felt like I had to go. Like I was supposed to go.

Ms. Homeyer died in the faculty bathroom during second period.

There was an ambulance and three police cars, and we watched through the windows during English as they rolled her body out on a stretcher.

Cynthia Roberts was in the faculty lounge stapling papers when it happened.

"She, like, let out this disgusting noise." Cynthia was telling the girls at the table next to me at lunch.

"What do you mean?" one of them said.

I stopped chewing my Doritos so I could hear better.

"It was like, this moan and then a thump," she said.

I felt sick to my stomach. Thump. She'd heard Ms. Homeyer die. She'd heard her go thump.

"Did you go in there?" the girl asked.

"*Eww* no."

I wanted to ask her a question too. I wanted to ask her if she felt anything. Did she feel something leaving. Something shifting. Something gone.

I looked across the table at Skeeter. He had his headphones on and was cutting his sandwich into little squares with his pocketknife.

We were the only two people at the table.

"Skeeter," I said.

He didn't look up.

"Skeeter."

He pulled off the bread on one of the squares and started cutting into the turkey.

I sat there. It was loud. People laughing. A lawn mower going. The low hum of the pop machines.

All around me books and clothes and windows and chairs and so many people. People everywhere and I sat there.

Someone was dead.

That afternoon, the more the news spread, the worse things got.

In history, this kid said, "Do you think she croaked before or after she took a dump?"

We were supposed to be looking over our homework but the room was loud. Mr. Tanner was at the front doing something on his iPad.

I tried to sit there and not say anything. I tried to not care.

Why should I care?

But everyone was talking about it.

I heard she had an attack and fell into the toilet.

I bet that was a pretty crappy way to go.

Hahahahahahahahahahahahahahahahahahaha.

I felt sweat start to bead up. I didn't want to do anything about it, but I also wanted them to shut their faces.

I closed my eyes and took three breaths. Slowly.

None of this mattered. Nothing mattered. Ms. Homeyer died on the toilet at Palo Verde High and it didn't matter.

• 10 •

The light turned green, and the bus started to pull away from the 7-Eleven.

Ms. Dead Homeyer smiled. She stood in the middle of the parking lot, and she was wearing her art smock and polyester pants. Her gray hair in her regular fat curls, her Naturalizer shoes. She was even holding her gigantic Mountain Dew mug that was on her desk every morning.

She took a sip of her drink and smiled.

I said, "Skeeter," but it was a whisper and he didn't hear. He was still talking and talking and talking.

"Skeeter," I said again.

Ms. Dead Homeyer held up her mug.

I felt throw-up burn and I swallowed it back down.

Was this real?

The bus started moving and Ms. Dead Homeyer got smaller and smaller and smaller.

For ten more blocks I sat there, paralyzed.

• 11 •

At the beginning of eighth grade, when we had lock-
ers and we were going to take oil painting and Gabby
had started being our friend, at the beginning of eighth
grade, we found out Kim's heart was taking a turn.

"What do you mean?"

Kim pulled yarn out of the afghan on my bed. "I mean
it's worse than it's ever been."

"Are you serious?"

"Yeah."

"Oh."

She threw a pillow at me. "Don't worry, I ordered
some books."

*　*　*

Kim ordered some books.

Life After Life: Survival of Bodily Death

Hello from Heaven: A New Field of Research-After-Death Communication Confirms That Life and Love Are Eternal

Reunions: Visionary Encounters with Departed

Talking to Heaven: A Medium's Message of Life After Death

She bought them on Amazon with Trish's credit card. Trish was going to kill her.

"She's going to kill you."

"I don't care," she said. "Her new boyfriend will make her feel better."

That was true.

We sat on Kim's bedroom floor and, before she opened the box, she said this, she said, "Promise me you won't laugh."

We were supposed to be studying for biology, and I looked at her.

"What?"

She cleared her throat. "I'm serious about this, Em. Promise me you won't laugh."

I sat on my hands so she wouldn't see that I was starting to shake.

"Promise me," she said again.

Kim never got like this.

"Okay," I said.

"Promise."

"I promise," I said.

She pulled the books out of the box.

"This one," she said, holding up *Reunions*, "this one was on the *Today Show*."

"So?"

"So. It's legit."

She turned it over and showed me the picture of the lady on the back. She had silver hair and yellow teeth and she was wearing a tiara.

Kim read the bio out loud: "'Tennesa Green, medium to the stars, shows readers in eloquent and insightful prose how easy it can be to communicate with their loved ones. Miss Green lives in Bowling Green, North Carolina, with her three cats, Prince, Princess, and Pea.'"

"Prince, Princess, and Pea?"

"I told you not to laugh," she said.

"I'm not laughing."

"Good because it's not funny."

"I know," I said. "It's not funny at all."

"If I had three cats that's what I would name them."

"I know," I said. "Totally."

"Totally," she said, and then we both started laughing.

She assigned me two books: *Hello from Heaven* and *Talking to Heaven: A Medium's Message of Life After Death*.

I was supposed to read them, take notes, and then report back.

When I got home, I put them in my underwear drawer and sat in the closet.

We didn't talk about the books again, and I thought it was over.

I hoped it was over. Most of the time I liked to pretend like nothing was wrong.

She was fine.

But then, a month later she called me and said this: "I found a real live medium trainer."

"What?"

"I found a guy."

"What?"

"Come over."

I sat on the phone for a second, trying to figure out what she was saying. She was talking fast and what?

"Come over."

It was ten on a school night.

"I can't."

"Of course you can."

"How?"

"Tell Joe to bring you."

I hesitated. Joe wouldn't drive me over there and really, I didn't want to go. The whole thing made me feel sick.

"Emmy?"

"What?"

"Tell Joe. It's important."

I walked across the hall to Joe's room. He was playing video games.

"Can you take me to Kim's?"

"No," he said.

"Please?"

"No."

"Why not?"

"Because I don't want to."

I stood there. "He won't take me," I said into the phone.

"Let me talk to him."

I gave the phone to Joe and he said, "What?"

Kim said something to him and he turned red. "Shut up," he said.

Then he started laughing.

"Fine," he said. Then he handed the phone back to me.

"Okay," she said.

"What?"

"He'll bring you."

I looked at him. He was back into his game, sniping guys in the water.

"What did you say to him?"

"Who cares?"

So Joe took me to Kim's apartment, and while he went to get some sunflower seeds at Smiths, I found out about Dr. Ted Farnsworth.

"Who?"

"Dr. Ted Farnsworth."

I sat on her bed and she scrolled down on the page.

"He's from Texas."

"So?"

"So my dad was from Texas."

I blew out some air. Trish told us that once. That Kim's dad was from Texas and he drove a Corvette. Blah blah blah.

Kim kept talking. "And this guy went to Harvard and look what it says, look."

I wished she would stop.

I wished she would just stop.

But I put on my glasses and started reading.

Dr. Ted Farnsworth is the leading expert in near-death experiences (NDE). He has documented thousands of NDE and is known for his theories on communication and the afterlife. In 1996, he developed a world-renowned program BEYOND TALKING that allows terminally ill patients to create a visitation path with their loved ones. Through proper training and preparation, the newly deceased can continue their relationships with the living.

Kim tapped the computer screen. "See?"

"What?"

"You really can talk to dead people."

Above the text was a picture of Dr. Ted Farnsworth.

He looked like a sixty-year-old trying hard to be a forty-year-old: his skin orange, his hair blond, a thick mustache, and bright white teeth because he was smiling. Hard.

"He looks creepy," I said.

"He does not look creepy," Kim said. "He looks professional."

She scrolled down. "Read this," she said, pointing to a testimonial.

> My husband passed away on Christmas Day. We knew it was coming and read Dr. Farnsworth's books beforehand. Thanks to Dr. Farnsworth, I have had the pleasure of talking to my Henry several times since his passing. This life is not the end! The program has changed both of our lives.
>
> —Cheryl Eastman

"Kim," I said, trying not to be mean, "there is no way this is true."

She wasn't listening. She sat on her foot now and said, "Read this one. Read this one."

> My daughter Barbie died unexpectedly. We were devastated but, through Dr. Ted's program, my wife and myself have both been able

to communicate with her. We can't thank Dr. Ted enough for the work he's done.

—Josh Timms

The next one was worse.

I love my boyfriend, and when he died I thought my life was over! I was so wrong. So so wrong. Dr. Ted Farnsworth's program is amazing! Life doesn't have to end when we die!!!!!!!!!

—Erica Stevens

My head started to ache. "I think Joe's back," I said.

She kept scrolling down, like she didn't hear.

Then she said, "He's coming to Vegas."

"What?"

"He's coming," she said. "It's not for months but that's okay. We'll have time to get ready."

She clicked on his events page.

Come meet Dr. Ted Farnsworth for yourself! Presenting his groundbreaking, life-changing, heartwarming work, Dr. Ted will be speaking about his program BEYOND TALKING at Circus Circus Resort in Las Vegas. Tickets are only $99.99 per person for this three-hour presentation and includes a copy of Dr. Ted's new bestselling book, *Crossing the Veil, How Death Does Not Need to Be the End*. February 12.

She turned and looked at me. "We have to go," she said.

I stared at her. "You're not serious."

"I'm totally serious." She turned back and clicked on his bio again. "I want to go," she said.

People used to talk about me and Kim.

They never fight. They never disagree. They never get jealous. It's like they were made for each other.

We were made to be best friends.

I used to be proud of that.

Nothing was ever wrong between me and Kim. Ever.

Until she decided to die.

12

In front of the bus outside the mortuary, the hot air rushed at me and I felt like my knees were going out.

I looked up the street.

I looked down the street.

We were on the outskirts of the city now. Desolate and palm trees. Everything brown and dirty.

"Are you okay?" Skeeter asked. He touched my arm. Then he took it away. Then he put it back. Then he took it away.

I looked at him. "What are you doing?"

I almost forgot I'd seen Ms. Dead Homeyer, he was acting so weird.

"Nothing," he said. "Nothing."

The mortuary was in a run-down strip mall. A neon sign said OPAL'S FAMILY MORTUARY. The *O* on the sign was burned out so it was really PAL'S FAMILY MORTUARY, which made me feel a lot better.

On one side of the mortuary was a Thai restaurant. On the other side was a Hairport.

There were three cars in the parking lot and one person.

The person was a redheaded skinny kid in a tank top, green Pumas, and he was sitting on the curb right in front of the mortuary.

His face was covered with zits, and I felt like I shouldn't look at him. I also felt like maybe I'd seen him before but I hadn't.

He sat on the sidewalk holding a slushie.

No Ms. Dead Homeyer.

"This place is an armpit," Skeeter said.

"Yeah," I said.

And then his phone rang.

"It's my mom," he said. "Hang on for one second." He walked over by the Thai restaurant to talk.

I had never been to a real mortuary. I'd never seen where they actually put the bodies. Where they take them.

My heart pounded.

A year ago tomorrow Kim died.

Friday, May 26th at 5:48. The date and time I'd written

over and over and over again in notebooks, inside book covers, on the wall of my closet.

A year ago tomorrow, at 5:48, my best friend died, and I'd just had a visitation from a dead lady.

Why? Why not you, Kim?

I took a breath.

Maybe she would be in the mortuary with Ms. Dead Homeyer. Maybe this was what I'd been waiting for.

The kid with the zits made a loud sucking sound with the straw. I ignored him.

A plane flew over and the kid said, "Do you know what time it is?"

I still acted like I didn't hear because I was thinking about dead bodies and he was annoying.

"Hey," he said. "What time is it?"

I put my hand to my forehead like I couldn't see him because it was too bright.

"Do. You. Know. What. Time. It. Is?"

He was wearing a watch.

He saw me look at it and said, "It's broken."

So I looked at mine. Kim's watch really. She'd given it to me along with her iPod, her set of Roald Dahl books, and her old American Girls dolls, which I didn't really want even though she had all of them. Even Marie Grace.

51

"Five forty," I said.

He stared at me. "What?"

"Five forty," I said again.

He took a few seconds and I thought maybe he was high, but then he said, "Oh. Thanks."

Then he said, "I already knew that. I knew it before you even said it," he said.

He slurped more on his straw. It was so loud it echoed.

Skeeter was still talking. I looked at the Hairport.

"That your boyfriend?" the kid said.

I looked at him. Why was he talking to me?

"What?"

"Is that kid your boyfriend?"

Skeeter, who one time when we were kids had to go to the ER because he ate carpet, lived in the next neighborhood down and at the moment he was my only friend. But he was not my boyfriend.

"No," I said.

Then he said, "But he likes you."

"No," I said. "No. He doesn't like me."

"Yeah, he does," the kid said, and I felt myself start to burn, which was stupid.

He didn't like me like that. No boys liked me like that.

"I can tell he's into you," the kid said.

"We Don't Like Each Other."

He still smirked but he said, "Okay. Okay. No big deal. I just thought you're so dressed up, must be a date."

He put his mouth back on the soggy straw.

"We're going there," I said, pointing to the mortuary.

The kid turned and looked.

"Oh. Bummer. Who died?"

Why was Skeeter taking so long?

"Who died?" he said again.

"My teacher."

"Your teacher?"

"My earth science teacher," I said.

He nodded. "You loved her?"

"No."

"You liked her?"

"No."

"Oh," he said.

Then he said, "Do you like burritos?"

"Uh," I said, trying to figure out how to get out of this conversation and maybe he was mentally disturbed and this was how he made human connections. "Uh, yeah. I like burritos."

He nodded. "I thought you might."

If Kim were here, she'd love this boy. She'd love how weird he was.

Skeeter started walking over then.

"I have to go," I told the kid.

He said, "As you should."

And that was it.

13

Kim and I, we used to ride our bikes up and down the street in my neighborhood. We'd wear her mom's costume wigs, and we'd ride with no hands and we'd yell things.

If a blue car drove by we'd yell, "Hey, morons! Go back to the sea!"

If a minivan drove by, we'd yell, "Babies ruin the world."

If a truck came by we'd yell, "Little Man Disease."

The whole thing was Kim's idea and at first I was like, "What?"

And she said, "Come on, Em. Please. I'm so bored."

"I don't think we should," I said, and she said, "Come on. It's not that big a deal." I was scared we were going to get arrested but I did what I always did. I took a big breath and said, "Okay."

We got our bikes, and she made me wear the clown Afro and she wore the Elvira wig. And then we put on these scarves *so that no one would be able to identify us*, Kim said. Which was a really good plan.

We rode our bikes, and trucks went by.

Cars went by, too, and we screamed our faces off.

At first, I was scared but then it started to feel good. It felt good to scream. To yell whatever came into my head and not care.

Once when a Pinto went by I yelled, "You're a bean!"

Kim was laughing so hard and so was I and it was stupid, but we both couldn't stop laughing and she said, "I told you," she said. "I told you, you'd like it."

Then . . .

This lowrider Cadillac drove by real slow, the window was down and there was base pounding, and the man filled up the whole seat. Like an overflowing bag of potato chips, and I got brave. I got too brave and shouted. I said, "Hey, fatbutt!"

The car braked in the middle of the road.

How could he have heard me? His rap music was up so loud, no way he heard me.

But he stopped. In the middle of the road.

And I panicked and stopped, too.

Kim said, "Crap," and I said, "Crap." And she said, "Ride away."

She rode her bike one way and I was trying to ride the other way, but I tripped on my shoes and I was trying to get back on and he was opening his door and I was sweating and I could hear Kim yelling, "Ride away, Em!" And right when I was almost riding away, I was almost riding away, the man, he was huge, a huge man with a belly and a long dark beard, he said, "Hey, you. Stop."

I tried to not stop. I tried to ride away and he said, "Stop or I'll beat your skull in."

So I stopped.

My heart was thumping and I stopped.

He said, "Turn around."

I turned around. He had on sunglasses, and he looked like a gang murderer and I was going to be murdered.

He walked right up to me. Right up to my face.

He said, "Did you just yell fatbutt at me?"

I started coughing and he said it louder, "Did you just yell fatbutt at me?" His breath smelled like soy sauce.

I said, "No, sir."

"Really? Because I heard you yell fatbutt at me."

I swallowed.

"Did you?" he said.

My stomach started to ache and I had to go pee and it was just him and me in the middle of the road.

"No," I said.

"You're lying."

I shook my head. "No. No, I'm not lying. I wouldn't yell something like that."

He cocked his head and I prayed. I prayed and prayed and prayed. I was going to be on *Dateline*, and he was going to kidnap me and put me in a cage.

He took a step closer to me, "You call me a fatbutt?"

I didn't know what to do and I was for sure going to die.

"Leave her alone."

Kim was back. She was on her bike and she still had on her wig and her oversized hot sunglasses that we bought two of at Claire's and she was holding a toy rake.

I almost started laughing because she was so tiny and

he was so huge, but then I was about to be murdered so I didn't.

She rode right up to us and stopped beside me. My heart started to slow.

The guy looked at her. "What did you say?"

"I said to leave her alone." Kim held the rake up.

"You gonna hit me with that?"

She said, "Maybe. You gonna make me hit you with it?"

He rubbed his face.

"You girls got problems."

"You got problems," Kim said, and I stood there. She was crazy.

The guy sighed. Then he walked over to his car and said, "This your lucky day, girlies. This is your lucky day."

Then he drove off.

Kim looked at me. I was soaked with sweat, trembling.

"I was so scared," I said, and Kim said, "So was I," and then we both started laughing.

• 14 •

The inside of the mortuary was a big minty green foyer with bad silk flowers, organ music, and a book that said, *In Remembrance.*

My sequin dress felt tight.

Skeeter was quiet. We both sort of stood there.

I looked back through the glass doors at the kid in the tank top. He was watching us.

I turned back around and tried to be a normal person. I am a normal person. Everything is fine and I am a normal person. That kid out there is a normal person. Skeeter is a normal person.

And Ms. Dead Homeyer is dead.

She is dead and I was tired. And maybe I hadn't seen her at the 7-Eleven. Maybe it was just my mind playing tricks on me.

But I also took a step away from Skeeter for no reason.

A guy in a plaid jacket with glasses said, "You can sign your names here."

He pointed to the book. "Go ahead," he said, and he had a long fingernail on his pinkie. This made me think he probably picked his nose.

Skeeter wrote his name.

I wrote mine.

There were only three other names in the book.

John Hardy.

Sharlene West.

And Al Au.

Al Au taught geography at our school, and I guess he was Ms. Homeyer's friend. He was from Hawaii and one time made me say *Aloha* into the microphone during an assembly.

My hands started to sweat.

"Why are there only three names," I whispered to Skeeter.

He shrugged.

"Are there only three people here?"

"I don't know," he said.

I felt panic. I felt panic all over. I thought there'd be a lot of people. I don't know why but I just thought, I thought that old ladies would have lots of people at their funeral. There were lots of people at Kim's. People from our neighborhood. From school. Her mom's friends. My parents' friends. And Kim was only fourteen.

I thought there'd be a lot of people at Ms. Homeyer's funeral, and no one would notice us.

Now. It was just me and Skeeter. And three other people. And one of them was Mr. Aloha.

It suddenly felt hard to breathe.

The man with the coat stared at us.

"Let's leave," I whispered.

Skeeter looked at me. It was my idea in the first place. I knew he was thinking that. I found the obituary. I googled the address. I got the bus route.

It was me. All of this was me.

"You want to leave?" he said.

"Yes."

"Why?"

"I feel sick," I said.

The man with the nose-picker fingernail said something to us, he said, "They're waiting for you."

We both turned and looked at him. "What?"

"I told them you were here. They're waiting for you."

"What are you talking about? Who is waiting for us?" Skeeter said.

The man smiled. Then he said, "They won't move the body into the chapel until you've had time to pay your respects."

• 15 •

Trish decided to cremate Kim.

Kim did not want to be cremated. She even told Trish that. She said, "No matter what you do, Mom. Don't cremate me."

Don't.

"But it was cheaper and then I could keep her with me all the time," Trish said, and she even offered to give me a Baggie full of ashes, but I said no thanks.

Trish put some of Kim's dead ashes in an Altoids tin and keeps Kim with her all the time.

I wondered if Trish planned the whole time to cremate her.

One time Kim and I found a bunch of pictures on the Internet of dead people put in interesting poses.

"What if they made me into a mannequin at Macy's?"

"What?"

"Like a dead mannequin. They'd get a lot of media coverage," she said.

"Yeah," I said. "They would but no one would shop there."

"I'd shop there," she said.

And she probably would but she can't because she's dead.

And when Mom told me Trish was going to burn Kim up, I thought I was going to puke. I sat in the bathroom for forty-five minutes and none of this was happening how it was supposed to happen. Nothing happened how it was supposed to happen and I had made a big mistake, and Kim was dead, and I couldn't tell her I was sorry. I'm sorry for everything. I'm sorry your mom is going to burn you up, and I'm sorry nothing happened the way it was supposed to happen, and I'm sorry I'm the worst friend ever.

When I finally came out of the bathroom, I got my copy of *Crossing the Veil.*

Dr. Ted Farnsworth said *cremation, embalmation,*

lost at sea, no matter what happens to your body, you can
still come back to see your loved ones. It was on page
thirty-five. Kim had circled it, which made me feel
better.

So Trish cremated Kim.

• 16 •

Skeeter and I followed the mortuary man into a room that had swaths of material stapled onto the wall. There was a white wicker archway, like at a wedding, but instead of a priest under it, there was a yellow casket with the lid up. We could barely see her nose. Her gray hair. Her hands on her chest.

We both stopped and stood there.

"Take your time," the man said.

Skeeter nodded and I thought I was going to really pass out now. I had just seen Ms. Homeyer in the parking lot and now she was in a box.

We walked up to her.

She was white and plastic and there was a teddy bear by her hip.

"This is weird," Skeeter whispered.

I nodded. "Uh-huh."

I couldn't stop looking at her face. Her face. She was sort of smiling, and one time I'd read that morticians sew their mouths that way. In a smile.

What if you didn't want to smile while you lay dead in a box? What if you didn't want them to sew you up or stuff you with jelly? Or like Kim, what if you didn't want them to burn you to dust?

"Come on," Skeeter said. "Let's get out of here."

He started to walk toward the door, but I couldn't leave.

"Wait," I whispered.

"What?" Skeeter said.

The guy was watching us from the doorway, his hands clasped, and I felt sick to my stomach but I also felt like touching her face.

My fingers started to tremble, and I knew that maybe I shouldn't touch her. I knew that maybe I'd get split personalities or something might happen. Something could happen. But I wanted to see what it felt like to be dead.

"What are you doing?" Skeeter said, his voice wobbly because he was a wimp sometimes.

68

"I just have to see."

"See what?"

My stomach churned.

I reached into the box. The man took a step forward; Skeeter took a step backward. I put my hand in the box, and right before I made contact, a chill ran through my body, a sharp, distinct chill. I took a breath and ran my finger over her cold dry lips.

The day before she died, in earth science, Ms. Homeyer
started crying.

Me and Skeeter were sitting at our desks watching the
Egypt video and doing word searches when it happened.

And Ms. Homeyer was crying.

Soft at first. Like a puppy.

Then it got louder.

Skeeter looked at me.

I looked at him.

"What should we do?" I whispered.

"We don't do anything," he said. Skeeter was smart
like me. He stayed out of things.

"We don't do anything?"

"No. What would we do?"

We both looked at her.

She had her head on her desk, and her shoulders were slumped.

Everyone else in the class was texting or playing games on their phones or sleeping.

"She wouldn't want us to do anything anyway," he said.

And I nodded. If I were mean and old and crying on my desk at school, I wouldn't want someone like me to do something.

I sat there and tried not to listen.

Even when her crying turned to sobs, small hiccupy sobs, no one turned to look.

I knew that something was wrong. Something was really wrong because Ms. Homeyer was not the type of lady to bawl at school. She usually just sat and watched soap operas on her computer.

I didn't want to do anything. I didn't want to do anything at all, but I couldn't not do anything.

"I'm going to see if she's okay," I whispered.

He looked up from his word search. If we did twenty word searches a week we got an A.

"Are you serious?" Skeeter said.

I swallowed. Was I serious? I turned and looked at her. I thought I was serious.

"She's probably fine," he said.

I knew why he was saying it. I knew why I shouldn't go over there.

It was a bad idea.

There are some teachers who you were supposed to talk to. Like Ms. Jensen, who has big boobs and used to be in *Wicked* in New York. Or Mr. Rencher, who brings pizza on Fridays and took his entire fifth period to *Mission Impossible*. There were teachers like that. Teachers I didn't talk to but I should talk to.

Then there were teachers like Ms. Homeyer.

"I'll just see," I said.

Skeeter nodded. "Okay."

The man on the video said, *they put the brains and innards in small containers called blah blahs.*

Someone yelled, "What about the balls!"

Everyone started laughing.

Homeyer didn't move, but the sobbing died down.

Skeeter looked at me.

I stood up. I had avoided things like talking to a teacher or getting out of my desk during class the entire year. I didn't like people looking at me. Or hearing me. Or seeing me.

But . . .

I walked to her desk and stood there for a minute.

She didn't move.

I looked at Skeeter. He shook his head.

I turned back to her and whispered, "Ms. Homeyer?"

She still didn't move.

I said it a little loud. "Ms. Homeyer?"

Nothing.

So I reached out, I reached out to touch her, even though I prefer not to touch anyone and especially not Ms. Homeyer. I reached out and poked her head.

She jumped and yelled, "What?"

The whole class turned.

"What?" she said again. Why was I standing there? Why was I doing this?

"Uh," I said. "Can I go to the bathroom?"

She waved me off and put her head back on the desk.

The next day she died.

• 18 •

After I touched Ms. Dead Homeyer, the whole world was moving and everything went black and I saw angels and they gave me some lip gloss.

Not really.

What happened was we went into the chapel for the funeral.

There were pews like at a church, but it felt different. The room was smaller and the walls were painted in the same mint color. And it was cramped. Like a mortuary dollhouse.

There were two old men sitting in the back. A little old lady in the front row and a man wearing a plaid jacket like the nose-picker guy.

In a corner sat a large woman in a muumuu with yellow hair. She was knitting something.

She turned and smiled at me like she knew me. Was she from school? Was she Au's wife? In any case, she was strange.

Music was playing from a CD player.

Skeeter said, "Are you sure you're okay?"

And I said, "Yeah."

And he looked at me and said, "Really?"

Right after Kim died, Skeeter brought me over a huge burned sugar cookie in the shape of a kangaroo. In the card it said, KEEP ON HOPPIN!

"My mom made it," he told me.

Our families had known each other for years, and Mom and Dad were always talking about Skeeter's deliquent brother.

He was in jail for a DUI, which was a horrible tragedy, my mom said once and Dad said, "A tragedy? He was drinking. He got in a car. That's called stupidity, not tragedy."

Mom said, "I know, Doug, but he didn't know better."

And Dad said, "What are you talking about?"

And then they argued and Mom said, "I feel bad for Sue."

✳ ✳ ✳

Sue was Skeeter's mom and Sue made me a kangaroo cookie when Kim died.

I said, "Thanks."

Skeeter said, "I had one of them. They don't taste good."

I said, "Okay."

Then he said, "Okay."

And then he left.

Now at Ms. Dead Homeyer's funeral he said, "Are you okay? Really?"

"I'm okay," I said.

We sat on the back pew next to the two old men.

A huge picture of Ms. Homeyer wearing her Smurf smock, holding a cat, was on an easel at the front.

Then the man from the foyer wheeled her casket to the front, and they changed the music to a song called "We Are the World."

We sat there.

And sat there.

And sat there.

Mr. Au went up and whispered to one of the mortuary guys.

Then we sat and sat and sat.

At six thirty, Mr. Au walked up to the microphone.

"Hello," he said, and the microphone feedback bounced off the walls.

The music went off.

"Sorry," he said. "Sorry about that."

Then a bell chimed signaling that someone had come in the mortuary. One of the mortuary guys left and Au said, "Today, I'm going to talk about a dear friend named Carla Homeyer."

He pointed to the picture.

Mr. Au was wearing the same thing he wore to school every day: a golf shirt and Bermuda shorts. He cleared his throat, "Carla," he said. "Carla Carla Carla. What to say about Carla."

He cleared his throat again.

"Carla was a friend to many," he said. "She loved her students and she truly believed that there was life beyond this universe."

I sank in my seat.

"This is bad," Skeeter whispered.

"Really bad," I said.

Then they walked in.

The worst people who could possibly walk in, walked in.

• 19 •

One day, the summer before all of this, the summer before Kim died, Mom was off at an insurance workshop, and Dad was in his study, and Joe was eating Styrofoam or playing the Wii, and Kim and I were in my room dying from sweat. Kim was on the floor staring at her feet and I was on the bed trying to see if I could put my entire fist in my mouth.

"You can't do it," she said.

"I think I can."

"No," she said. "It's physically impossible. Besides you're a weirdo."

"It's not physically impossible," I said. I tried again, and she was probably right.

Then she said, "Why do you have so many stuffed animals?"

I looked over at the corner of the room. My mom had helped me rig up a net to hold all the toys I'd gotten over the years. My grandma was crazy town, and me and Joe each got three stuffed animals for every holiday.

"I love them," I said.

She looked at me. "You do?"

"No."

She sat up. "I think we need to set them free."

I got nervous. Kim had a lot of ideas. In third grade I got grounded because Kim had decided to put gelatin in all the toilets.

"What do you want to do?"

She smiled. "It's going to be epic," she said.

"What?"

"Trust me," she said.

I sighed.

So we got a bunch of trash bags and gathered all the animals in the house. My room, the rec room, we even went into Joe's secret area of his closet and filled two bags.

"He's going to kill us," I said.

"He can't kill us," she said. "He's a baby."

And she was right. Joe was a baby.

We lugged them all out to the curb, making four trips.

"Your grandma is insane," Kim said.

"I know."

Then we started sticking the animals to the light pole with duct tape.

"Why are we doing this?"

"Because it's important," Kim said, taping my Elmo on first.

I watched her. Then I said, "We should do it by color."

"What?"

"By color."

I figured if we were going to do something like this, might as well be organized about it.

Kim shrugged. "Okay."

So she taped and I handed her toys.

We started with Mr. Polar Bear and Joe's pair of bunnies and then we moved from white to gray with Hippy Hippo and a couple of elephants we got from the San Diego Zoo one time.

An hour later we had stacked two chairs on my dad's folding table.

"I'm almost out of tape," Kim said. "Maybe you should go ask Gabby for some?"

We both looked across the street. Gabby Forster lived in the biggest house on the block. Gabby always wore bikinis, she never rode bikes or played night games, and one time she told us that her family's beach house sometimes got rented by Jean-Claude Van Damme.

So she was way cooler than us.

Right then, while we were staring at her house, Gabby walked out.

She was wearing a hot pink bikini, and she looked like a model.

"What are you guys doing?" She yelled across the street, which was shocking. Like she cared.

Kim taped a tiger next to Winnie-the-Pooh. "We're protesting stuffed animal cruelty," she yelled back.

I tried not to laugh. Gabby scared me. Nobody scared Kim.

Gabby walked over. "What are you doing?"

I held a leopard up to Kim.

"We're making a statement," Kim said.

"Yeah, we wanted to make a statement," I said, which was exactly what Kim just said.

Gabby stared at the pole. "You guys are strange," she said.

I wanted to say something like *this was Kim's idea*. I would never do this. I was not strange, I was normal. I am normal and cool, too. But instead I didn't say anything.

Then Gabby said, "Why are you doing this again?"

"Tell her, Emmy," Kim said.

I looked at her. "What?"

"Tell her why we're doing this."

"Uh." I hated when Kim put me on the spot. "Uh."

"Don't hold back," Kim said. "We want the people to know."

"Uh," I said again. "We are concerned that stuffed animals are being . . .

"Uh . . .

"Stuffed animals are being treated unfairly?" I said. This was so dumb. We were so dumb.

But Kim said, "Exactly. It's atrocious."

"Oh yeah," Gabby said, a hand on her bony hip.

Kim stopped taping. "For example, Gabby, where are your stuffed animals?"

"What?"

"Like right now."

"Uh, I don't have any stuffed animals."

Kim pointed a leopard at her and said, "Now that's a lie. That is a horrible horrible lie. Statistics show that ninety-eight percent of the population has at least one stuffed animal in their bedroom. If not in their bedroom, within twenty feet of their bedroom."

Where did she come up with this stuff?

Gabby said, "Well I don't."

Kim gave her this look she does, like the time Joe lied to us and told us there were no more brownies, and she did the look and he turned red and she said, where are the brownies and he said they're gone and she did the look harder and then he said, just don't eat them all and pulled them out from under the sink.

It was her lie look.

"What are you doing?" Gabby said to Kim.

Kim kept giving her the look.

"What is she doing?" she asked me.

I shrugged.

Then, like magic, Gabby said, "I have some stuffed animals."

Kim nodded. "See? Ninety-eight percent of the population."

We went back to taping and Gabby stood there. I tried not to keep looking at her. Why was she out here?

After a few minutes she said, "Do you want to use my dad's Little Giant ladder?"

Kim smiled. "We need more duct tape, too," Kim said, and Gabby ran home.

That afternoon we covered the pole as high as the Little Giant ladder could go. Gabby brought out a bin full of Beanie Babies.

We even got more stuffed animals from some of the other neighbor kids.

When we were almost done, a Jeep full of boys pulled up.

Gabby, who was holding up a hot pink rhino, immediately dropped it and walked over.

"Hey, guys," Gabby said, leaning into the Jeep.

How did she know how to be so sexy?

The driver, a beautiful boy with dark hair, ignored Gabby and yelled to Kim, "What are you doing up there?"

Kim looked down. "What?"

"What are you doing up there?"

I looked at Kim. He was talking to her. He was looking at her. She was thirteen. Almost fourteen but still, she was thirteen, and he had to be at least sixteen.

"I'm eating tacos. What are you doing?" Kim said.

He laughed.

Gabby said, "I have no idea what they're doing. It's so lame."

The kid cut her off and said to Kim, "Will you come do that at my house?"

Kim said to me, "Emmy. Can I have that unicorn?"

I handed her the unicorn, my hand trembling, I don't know why.

"You playing hard to get?" he said.

Gabby tried to talk to them again but the kid kept not paying attention to her and I kept feeling sick to my stomach and Kim kept taping animals.

Finally they drove away.

Gabby stalked back to the pole and sat on the curb.

Thirty minutes later we had no more animals.

Kim came down from the ladder, and we all stood in the road to look at it.

"Wow," Gabby said.

Kim nodded. "It's beautiful."

"It's better than beautiful," I said.

Then Joe came out. "What the crap are you guys doing?"

Dad followed him out.

"Dad, look what Emmy and Kim did."

Dad stared at it.

Joe stared at it. We were all staring at it.

Kim said, "Joe, You know you love it."

And he said, "It's stupid," and then he said, "Hey is that my . . ."

Then he stopped because Gabby was standing there, and Joe had had a crush on her since she told him he looked like a UFC Fighter and clearly a UFC Fighter wouldn't own a Shamu doll.

He stopped and we all stood there.

It was the weirdest thing we had ever made, but it was also the best thing. Almost the best thing.

We left the animals up there for a week. People came from all over to see it, and we even got a small article in the newspaper:

GIRLS MAKE HUMANITARIAN STATEMENT ABOUT STUFFED ANIMALS

There's a picture of the pole and me, Kim, and Gabby, our arms around one another's shoulders like we all belonged together.

• 20 •

Two days after the stuffed animal light pole, Gabby showed up on our porch.

Kim and I were on the swing eating Cheetos, discussing whether it would be worth it to sit on a couch for a year if you got a million dollars when it was over.

Gabby had no shoes on and she wore a gold bikini. She said, "What are you guys doing?"

I looked at Kim. This was so weird. All these years across the street and she hardly ever even looked at me, let alone came over to talk.

"Gabby," Kim said, "if someone told you that they'd

give you a million dollars if you sat on a couch for a year, would you do it?"

My stomach knotted. Another dumb conversation. She was going to think we were so stupid.

She leaned against the railing and said, "What?"

Kim held the Cheetos out for her, which I was sure she wouldn't eat.

"Think carefully," Kim said. "Would you sit on a couch for a year for a million dollars?"

Gabby took the bag and said, "Where is the couch? Like in my front room?"

Kim nodded. "It's wherever you want it to be. Your room. Your kitchen. Backyard."

Gabby pulled out a handful of Cheetos, and we were in the twilight zone.

"Can it be a sectional?"

"No," Kim said. "Just a regular couch."

"Can you exercise on it?"

"You just have to always be touching it," I said, getting up my courage. "But you can do jumping jacks or lift weights."

Kim and I had worked all this out.

"Huh," she said. "What about the bathroom?"

We went through all the scenarios and soon she was

on the swing with us. She'd only do it if she could get the couch from some furniture store I'd never heard of. And she wanted it reupholstered every three months, but how would she do that? Then she said the kicker. She'd have to have at least four people on staff the entire year.

"For what?" I asked.

"Uhhh, basic human needs. Duh."

I swallowed. "How would you pay them? It'd have to come out of the million dollars," I said because it would.

She gave me a dirty look. "No way. I get the million after. This is part of the deal."

"What? It's not a couch and a couple of servants. It's just a couch."

I couldn't believe I was arguing with her but hello. "You can't have a staff for free."

"You never said that in the beginning. The only stipulation was that you had to be touching a couch for a year," Gabby said.

"Yeah but . . ." and on and on and on. Gabby was so stubborn and it made me mad. You can't make up your own rules. It was our game.

Finally, when we were both almost shouting, Kim yelled "HEY!"

We stopped.

"Gabby can have a staff."

"WHAT?"

Gabby smiled.

"But does it come out of the million?"

"No," Kim said. "You were the one who said it was okay to have movers take you and the couch to the movies and restaurants, and we never said that had to come out of the money."

I folded my arms. "That's different."

"It's not different," Gabby said.

"It's not different," Kim said, and I was mad. I scooted over to the end of the swing.

Gabby stood up. "Do you guys want to come swimming? We just got a new slide, and my mom went to Costco and we have a ton of good food."

Kim looked at me. "That'd be fun," she said.

"Ugh." I didn't want to go swimming. Ugh.

They both stared at me. "Sure," I finally said.

And so we went swimming at Gabby's, who gets to have a staff of four if she ever lives on a couch for a year.

21

The worst people possible walked into Ms. Dead Homeyer's funeral.

First Gabby.

She was wearing tight tiny shorts and a tank top. Her boobs were showing, which meant she was wearing the double padded bra she ordered online from Bonanza dot com last summer. She made me get one, too, but it didn't do that to my chest.

"You should get one, Kim," she'd said.

Kim just laughed. Kim didn't need a bra to do stuff to her chest.

Now Kim was dead.

So Gabby was wearing that bra for sure, her hair in a ponytail, and green eye shadow.

I pulled my jacket closed over my sequin dress and acted like I didn't care.

Then two of Gabby's halter-top friends, Sadie Andreason and Heidi Baker, came in.

Next was Jud Jackson and Paul Lohner and Carl Armstrong. Then Laura Thomas and Jillie Brown.

And then, as if things couldn't get any worse, the hugest jerk of all of them, Tony Shurtz.

When Tony Shurtz walked in, I wanted to die. I couldn't deal with him today. Not today.

I sank in my seat even lower.

Skeeter looked at me. "What are you doing?"

I was so far down on the pew, I couldn't see Mr. Au. In fact, my head was cranked into my chest.

"What are you doing?"

"Nothing."

"Nothing?"

"Nothing," I said.

Mr. Au got out a ukulele and started singing.

By the time he was done with his song about birds, ten more people in our grade had walked in.

I sat up. What is going on?

Finally, after one more song, this one about dogs, Au put his mouth on the mic. "That was a song I know Carla liked." He wiped his forehead, because singing songs with a ukulele can get sweaty and said, "We don't have anything else planned for the funeral, right?"

He looked at the mortuary guys. They looked at each other.

Who was in charge? Where was Ms. Homeyer's family? Where were her friends?

Au said, "I thought we could have an open microphone. Anyone who feels compelled to should come up here and express their feelings."

An open mic? At a funeral?

For no reason, my heart started to thump.

He kept talking, "I see that some of my homeroom students are here. They were a half hour late and that was my fault. I told them the wrong time."

Tony Shurtz fake laughed, loud and obnoxious, and I thought I would throw up. I was sure I would throw up.

Au kept talking, "You only get tardy makeup points if you come say something about Ms. Homeyer. Aloha."

And then he sat down.

Mr. Au was giving out tardy makeup points for talking at Ms. Dead Homeyer's funeral?

Perfect.

I looked back at Tony, and he winked at me.

After Mr. Au opened the funeral up, everyone sat there.

The lady knitting in the corner sneezed so loud the light flickered.

She had really, really yellow hair.

And then it was silent again.

Au turned around and looked at all of us.

"Go up there," he said. His voice boomed, almost shaking the pews.

Someone giggled.

I thought you shouldn't yell at people during a funeral, but obviously I didn't know anything.

I looked over at Gabby.

When she saw me looking at her, I looked away.

"Do you want to leave?" Skeeter whispered.

"It's okay," I said. I didn't want to walk out in front of everyone, have them all watch me.

But the room was closing in. Everything was getting tighter and smaller. I felt dizzy, so I focused on watching the muumuu lady's hair in the light. The dust particles in the air moving in and out of the bleached strands.

Au turned around again. "Tony," he said. "You need some points. Get up there."

Why Tony? Why was this happening?

Tony said, "Me? Me?" in a loud voice that echoed off the walls.

"Yeah, Tony. Come on," Au said.

Tony stood up, his Knicks jersey and all. His friends patting him on the back. "Go, Tony," one of them said.

I hated this. This was a funeral.

A funeral.

He sauntered up to the front and stood at the podium.

He stood there for a while saying nothing, and people were whispering-giggling. He looked over at me and winked. I felt like I'd been kicked.

Finally he said in a fake crying voice, "I've been really struggling with Ms. Homeyer's death. She was like a mother to me."

They giggled. Giggle giggle.

Skeeter stared at him.

Tony kept talking. "Carla, she always wanted me to call her Carla, she one time held me like a baby, and I found comfort in her bosom."

I waited for Au to tell him to stop, but he didn't. He just let him keep going. Like this whole thing was a joke.

"When she died, a part of me died with her."

He looked at the casket, "Me and Carla forever," he said, and then he blew a kiss at the box.

Someone laughed. Loud.

Au turned around and gave whoever it was a look. That was it.

Tony walked back to his seat, smiling at me.

My stomach rumbled.

22

Tony Shurtz was the type of person who made you want to hide in the janitor's storage room.

He was a huge kid with a big face and spiky black hair, and he wore NBA jerseys every day. Usually the Knicks but sometimes the Spurs or the Lakers and he was nasty nasty mean.

Like one time he made my English teacher, Mrs. Porter, bawl when he glued her purse closed while she was in the bathroom.

One time he got this picture of a girl in my class, Laurel Preston, and he pasted a photo of a pig on her face and put it up all over the school. From then on, people oinked like a pig when Laurel walked by.

And he made everyone laugh during class by saying disgusting things. Like when Mindy Chapman was doing her report on ancient China and she was wearing white pants, and he kept asking questions like, what PERIOD was the Great Wall made, and do you think this PERIOD in history was important to women? And do you think women during this PERIOD would have rode on donkeys or would it have irritated them?

Everyone knew what he was doing, and the teacher was sitting there in oblivion.

Mindy had had a mishap a couple of months before.

Tony was nasty.

But the worst part about Tony was the entire year, this year, when I wanted no one to look at me. No one to talk to me. I just wanted to be alone and sit there. This year, he'd picked me.

He picked me.

Every day on the bus, and he'd walk by, he'd whisper something. Something like, *How's your dead friend?*

Or

Are you sad the only reason people talked to you is gone?

Or

You look especially fat today, Emmy. Too bad you don't

have your good-looking friend around to make you feel better.

Sometimes in the hallway he'd yell something at me

And it wasn't even obvious how horrible it was. Like he'd say, "HEY, EMMY! HOW ARE YOU!"

And everyone would turn and look at me. I hated everyone looking at me.

Or he'd go, "EMMY! DID YOU GET THAT SHIRT AT T.J. MAXX? IT LOOKS AMAZING!"

It'd always be when I looked like crap because I always looked like crap.

I tried to not care. I tried to breathe and not care.

Don't care.

Who cares.

But he was there. Always.

Before Kim died, he was just an obnoxious kid. After she died, he turned into this monster that was in every hallway. Every class. Every lunchtime.

I didn't get it.

One time, I was out in the deserted hall during pre-algebra to take a note to the office for my teacher. It had been a bad day already. I hadn't slept all night, Mom had made me drink a green smoothie for breakfast, and then I'd forgotten I had to give a report on van Gogh in history.

It was just a sucky day. And then, I saw Tony.

He was at the other end of the hallway, right by the office where I had to go.

I stopped.

I could . . .

What could I do?

I could turn around.

I could go around the school outside.

I could . . .

I could go in the bathroom and wait, but I was supposed to hurry.

I could . . .

What could I do? How could I avoid this?

But he had already seen me. He had seen me and he was walking toward me. I went to the side of the hall and looked at the ground as I walked.

Pleasepleasepleasepleasepleaseplease-pleaseplease-pleasepleasepleaseplease.

His footsteps got louder, almost exaggerated and, of course, they were exaggerated; he was stomping but I wouldn't look up. I had to walk fast and get past him. Just walk fast and get past him.

Then he was standing there, in front of me.

"Hi, Emmy," he said.

He was wearing basketball shorts with a huge hole. And his dumb Knicks jersey.

"Hi," I said. I took a step to go around, but he blocked me.

"Where are you going?"

"To the office," I said, all quiet.

"What?"

"To the office," I said.

"I can't hear you."

My stomach rumbled.

"I'm going to the office," I said, and I looked at his face for the first time. He had a big smile and he'd been sunburned, his face on one side was blistered and bulging.

"Will you let me go?" I said.

He nodded. "Sure," he said. "Go ahead."

I took a step, but he blocked me again.

I took a step the other way. He did it again.

I tried to run the other way.

He did, too.

Back and forth and back and forth

And he said, "This is fun, Emmy."

I stopped.

He stopped.

Then he said, "Did you ever know that everyone talks about how unfortunate your body is?"

My heart pounded. Pounded. And I just wanted to be nowhere. I just wanted him to leave me alone.

"Please let me go," I said.

"Be my guest," he said. And he leaned in, right up to my face, his breath hot and stale, and was about to say something when Mrs. Taylor came out of classroom and headed toward the office.

I stepped around Tony and followed the teacher.

Tony didn't do anything, except he did whistle. A soft low whistle that made my hair stand up.

And I hated him.

I hated him and I hated school and I hated everything.

23

The open mic continued. People really wanted tardy makeup points.

Some people talked about how Au did a really cool luau at lunch last month and how that was cool and everything's cool, and Ms. Homeyer died and she would have been sad because she's going to miss more cool luaus.

Some people talked about how they did all their word searches in Ms. Homeyer's class and how they learned so much when they finally found the words Red Giant.

Some people said sort of sincere things like, Ms. Homeyer was a nice lady or Ms. Homeyer had a good smile.

One kid, Josh Ahlstrom, he put his mouth on the microphone and said, "Au. You the man."

He fist-pumped.

Au said, "All right, all right."

And he said, "No seriously, you the man."

I hoped Au didn't give him points for that, but he probably would because he the man.

One old guy got up and said she was good neighbor. The other old guy knew her from Bingo, which made me feel even worse for her. She wasn't that old. Why was she going to Bingo? Suddenly I knew I was going to play Bingo like Ms. Homeyer some day. When I was twenty-five or twenty-six, and I was going to die alone.

The last person to get up other than me and Skeeter was Gabby.

The whole time people had been talking, she'd just sat there. I kept stealing looks at her. And even with all the makeup, she looked pale. Almost sick and I wondered if she remembered what day it was tomorrow.

I wondered if she was thinking about Kim, too.

After Byron Smith, she stood up.

She was wearing one of my headbands that I'd left at Kim's house and for some reason that made me feel hopeful. I don't know why.

Gabby had the capacity to surprise you.

She walked up the aisle. Slow.

She looked at me.

I looked at my hands.

She stood at the microphone.

"I think it's sad Ms. Homeyer died," she said.

Au nodded.

"I think . . .

"I think . . ."

Her voice cracked. She wiped her eyes and I couldn't believe it.

I waited, like everyone else, to hear what she was going to say next.

She took the microphone off the stand like she was going to do karaoke and said, "Ms. Homeyer, you did not have to die alone. None of us do, people. So love each other. Give someone a hug today."

Then she stopped.

Someone clapped.

We don't have to die alone.

We don't have to die alone.

We don't have to die alone.

I felt tears starting to form, but I blinked them away.

• 24 •

Kim's funeral had been at the Family Church for All People just off the strip. It was a dark place with stained-glass windows and hard black pews and a fat man in a suit who said things like Jesus loves you and Heaven is a place on Earth and Bless this Mess. Except he didn't say that but he probably would have.

Trish had come over right after Kim died. Like the night Kim died and she was crying and Mom was rubbing her back and Dad was walking around taking things out of cupboards and putting them back and Joe had his hat pulled down over his eyes.

I sat there.

I sat there waiting for Mom to look at me. For her to look at me and for me to be her horrible child, because I was horrible.

Everything was a blur. A horrible terrible blur.

I sat there and Kim was dead.

She was dead.

When we left the hospital I hadn't thought everything through but now I had and I hated myself.

"Is she in a drawer?" I said.

Everyone looked at me.

"What?" Trish said. Mascara was down her face, and she wiped her nose with her hand.

"Is she in a drawer?" I said again.

"Emmy," Mom said, "what has gotten into you?"

I sat there and they started talking again. I thought maybe Kim was in a drawer.

"They told me this could happen. We knew this could happen, right?" Trish said.

Mom nodded.

"I just, I just, you know, I didn't know, I didn't think."

She stopped and put her head on Mom's shoulder.

I thought about how Kim was in a drawer. At the hospital morgue.

I also thought about how I was a sucky friend.

Trish was talking again. She said her boyfriend was taking care of everything.

Mom said, "What do you mean?"

Trish always had new boyfriends. Kim never wanted to go home because Trish was never there and when she was there, she usually had a different guy with her. Her latest boyfriend, Greg, was a real estate agent with a huge head and a huge truck and a huge ego.

"He knows everyone," Trish said to me and Mom at a barbecue. Greg was telling Dad about a guy he knew who could help us fix the fence, and Kim said, "He doesn't know everyone, Mom."

Trish was annoyed. "He knows the guy who owns the Bellagio. He knows Siegfried. He knows Criss Angel."

"Gross," Kim said.

Then they got in an argument and Mom said, "Okay okay."

So now Greg the boyfriend real estate agent was taking care of everything.

"His brother knows a church and he said it's big and beautiful, right off the strip," Trish said. "They're going to help me with the expenses and Greg says they'll, you know, they'll make all the arrangements."

Mom said, "That's good."

"Yeah, it's a huge relief."

Joe looked at me and I looked at him.

One time, when the three of us—me, Joe, and Kim—were out in the pool, Kim had said, "What do you want your funeral to be like?"

She did stuff like that. Everything would be normal and then suddenly *what do you want your funeral to be like?*

She and Joe were playing a game of one-on-one and I was sitting on the steps keeping score. Joe was winning.

He said, "I'm not going to die."

He shot the basketball and it went in.

"Everyone dies," Kim said, grabbing the ball.

"Not me," Joe said. He was two years older than us and thought he was awesome.

"You're going to die, Joe. Sorry to say. And if you don't plan now, you'll be sorry."

She sounded like a commercial.

"Let's stop talking about this please," I said.

Kim tried to get around Joe, and there was splashing as he dunked her, and she shoved him and then she almost got to the basket, but he pulled her back under the water. She came up laughing.

"FOUL!" she said.

"Whatever."

"It was a foul," I said.

He handed her the ball, and she said, "For the record, I want my funeral at Red Rock."

Joe splashed her face, and she said, "Stop. I'm serious. Stop."

Joe stopped.

"Look at me," she said. She pointed at Joe and then at me. "Both of you. I want it at Red Rock. Maybe up Turtlehead Peak."

"Really?" Joe said. "That's the worst hike."

"I don't care," she said. "It's my funeral."

Joe glanced at me. Then he said, "Mine's going to be at the Thunderdome."

Barf. Of course.

"You could never fill the Thunderdome," I said. Because he couldn't.

"I could. I have fifty-five thousand friends and they'd probably put it on YouTube."

We started arguing and then Kim said, "GUYS!"

And we both got quiet.

"I'm serious. I want mine up Red Rock Canyon." She focused on me. "And I want live music and a chocolate fountain and buckets and buckets of Snickers bars and balloons. Hundreds of balloons."

Joe looked at me. I felt hot.

"You got it?" she said. "That's what I want."

Everything was quiet in the backyard then.

"You're a dork," Joe said, and grabbed the ball from her.

She was a dork and now she was dead and Trish's new boyfriend Greg was going to take care of everything. Kim hated Greg.

Joe kept giving me a look, so I said, "Kim wanted it at Red Rock."

"What?" Trish said. And then again, everyone was looking at me.

"She wanted her funeral at Red Rock."

"She talked to you about that?" Trish said.

I nodded. "She wanted it at Red Rock, and she wanted a live band and a chocolate fountain and Snickers."

Trish wiped her nose again.

"What?"

"A chocolate fountain."

"And balloons," Joe said, looking at me. "Remember? Hundreds of balloons."

Three days later, her funeral was at the Family Church for All People just off the strip. And it was huge. And dark. And Kim would have hated it.

Joe and I sat in between Mom and Dad

Kim's uncle kept hiccupping.

Gabby was in a maxi-dress that had birds on it.

The speaker was the fat man with the suit, and he talked about Daniel and the lions' den and love and one time, when he was up in a mountain all by himself, he had a vision, and in that vision he saw a young deer, a fawn. And the fawn came up and ate a peanut butter sandwich right out of his hand and, if you can believe this folks, he even nestled right up to the preacher. Like a deer hug. He said, "This deer gave me a hug and when I came to, when the vision ended and I was hiking down through the good trees of glory, I came upon none other than the dead carcass of a deer. A little deer. A fawn, ladies and gentlemen."

I stared at the box of ashes on the table in front.

The man spoke for forty-five minutes.

Then we sang a hymn about the beauty of the earth, and then it was over.

There was no chocolate fountain. No Snickers. No live bands. And no balloons.

Sometimes, I close my eyes and try to be nowhere. To feel what it would be like to disappear into the darkness.

What would it be like to be nowhere?

To be nothing?

It's easier to imagine than I want it to be.

• 25 •

There are points in my life where I do things that I shouldn't do or don't do things that I should.

Most days I don't do them, like when I saw Carlisle Peterson in my fifth period get Coke dumped on his head, and Mr. Bates looked up and said is anything wrong, and no one said anything, and Carlisle had soda all over his hair and face, and I knew I should say something, I knew I should, but I didn't.

Most days I'm like that.

But some days, even though I know it will turn out bad for me, like when Ms. Homeyer was crying or the time my dad got called a butthead at Joe's basketball game, there are times I can't sit still. Something inside me, or something outside of me, won't let me ignore what is happening.

At Ms. Dead Homeyer's funeral, after Gabby sat down, despite everything in my body telling me not to, at Ms. Dead Homeyer's funeral, I stood up.

I stood up.

Skeeter said, "Emmy, what are you doing?"

I tripped over his legs so I could get by, and people laughed and the yellow-haired lady was smiling so big her face was about to fall off.

I could do this. I could do this. I could do this.

I walked up to the podium and right when I got there I started to feel woozy.

I had something I wanted to say.

For twelve months, I'd been quiet. Almost every day since Kim died.

Now, at Ms. Homeyer's funeral, I wanted to say so many things.

I wanted to say, you guys are jerks.

I wanted to say, someone died. Did you know someone died? Someone is dead. You can't talk like that.

I wanted to say, don't you get bored? Don't you get tired? Doesn't it get old, making fun of people? Laughing at people?

I wanted to say, my best friend is gone and she told me she was going to come back. She promised me she would come back and visit me. You all have each other. You all have your stupid lives and I have nothing.

I wanted to say, I am so sad.

And finally I wanted to say, this is my mom's dress and I would never wear it in real life.

I stood there.

They were all were watching me. Gabby had that face on her face.

I swallowed and I was sweating, drips running down my back. Gabby leaned over and said something to one of her halter-top friends. The girl smiled.

They were doing it right in front of me and I stood there and I prayed.

I prayed to Kim. My best friend who saved me. She always saved me. I said: Dear Kim. Please. Please save me.

That's when Ms. Dead Homeyer walked in the door.

• 26 •

A week after Kim's funeral, Gabby came over.

She rang our doorbell and I was under my bed.

Mom let her come up to my room, which was about two feet high with clothes and old dishes.

Mom said, "Emmy?"

I didn't move.

"Em?"

They walked in. I watched Mom's feet, her Nike running shoes. Gabby was wearing flip-flops and her toenails were glitter pink. Because Gabby loves glitter.

I decided to see how long I could hold my breath but then I changed my mind and said, "I'm under here."

Mom squatted down. "What are you doing?"

"Lying under my bed."

"Come out from under there," Mom said. And I could tell she was embarrassed. My mom gets embarrassed about things like me lying under my bed.

I closed my eyes for three seconds.

Then I crawled out.

"Are you okay?" Mom asked.

"Yeah," I said.

Mom moved my hair out of my face. Then she said, "Your good friend Gabby is here."

Gabby stood against the wall, blending into the white paint almost. I'd never seen her look so bad and it sort of made me feel good. Which is mean.

"Okay," I said.

"I'll leave you two alone."

I sat on my bed.

I had worn the same clothes five days in a row, my hair was a knot, and I smelled like potato chips.

Gabby stood there and I sat there.

Then she said, "I brought you something." She handed me a box wrapped in polka-dot-pink paper with a silver bow.

"It's nothing really," she said. "It's not really any-thing. It's just, I just, I just thought . . . I don't know."

I held it in my hands and her voice thinned out to nothing.

Finally she said, "You can open it."

"Oh," I said. "Yeah."

The air felt hot and stale, and she kept playing with her T-shirt with a tiger on it that she got at Forever 21 because I was there sitting in the dressing room with her and Kim and she'd said, do you think I should get the tiger or the lion and Kim said tiger and I said lion.

She kept playing with her tiger shirt. Wadding it up and then letting it go. Her bones were small. Like a bird. I hadn't noticed before. I hadn't noticed a lot of things before.

I pulled the ribbon off and then opened the box.

Inside was a pillowcase with a deer in a cluster of trees embroidered on it.

"It's the deer from the story," she said.

I stared at it

"You know," she said, "from the funeral?

The deer from the funeral.

"Oh," I said.

"I made it myself," she said. "I mean, my mom helped me. But I did most of it. That's why his nose is sort of screwed up."

I looked at her.

"It's stupid," she said.

I didn't say anything.

"It's pretty stupid," she said.

The deer had a halo on it.

"Anyway," she said, "you can just throw it away."

I still didn't say anything because I didn't know what to say.

So then she said, "Are you going to that party Samantha is having?"

"What?"

"That party," she said.

"What party?"

She said, "You know. We were all going to go."

Once upon a time me and Kim and Gabby were going to go to some party at Samantha Ryland's house that she had every year, and I didn't want to go but it was always so huge and tons of high school people would probably be there and it was going to be A Mazzzzzzing.

I said, "No."

Kim said, "Maybe we should."

Gabby said, "Everyone's going to be there."

Kim looked at me.

"We'll do makeovers and look really hot and it's going to be so fun," Gabby said.

"We should go," Kim said again.

And I said, "Okay."

But that was five thousand years ago but really a month and Kim was in an Altoids box now and Gabby said, "I think we should still go."

I felt everything inside me tense up.

"You want to go to a party?" I said.

"No," she said. "I *am* going to a party and I think you should go with me."

I sat there.

She stood there.

"Emmy. Do you want to go?"

"No."

"You don't?"

"No."

"You should."

"No."

She stared at me. "Everyone is sad, Emmy."

I said, "Good one."

She bit her lip and then turned around and left.

• 27 •

There were a lot of things I could do. There were a lot of choices I could make.

And then there were some I couldn't make.

Like when I was standing at the podium at Ms. Dead Homeyer's funeral and she walked across the room, past her dead body and right up to my face where she almost kissed my cheek but instead said, "Hi, Sugar."

"Hi," I whispered.

She had never called me Sugar in real life. Not in a million years times a thousand. She seemed much more cheery now that she was dead.

She smelled like Mountain Dew and stale perfume, which

might be how death smells or maybe just Ms. Dead Homeyer. I couldn't be sure.

She smiled. Then she said, "They can't see me."

"What?" I said.

"They can't see me. You're looking at nothing right now."

And then I realized, I realized what she was saying, and it was true everyone was staring at me like I was crazy. I was crazy.

She said, "Just perk up and say what I say."

My heart was thumping. Just perk up and say what I say?

She cleared her throat and then she started speaking into my ear.

"Tell them I used to dance on the weekends," she said.

I looked at her. "What?"

"Don't talk to me, honey." She nodded toward the pews. I looked out and people were snickering.

"Say it," she said. "Tell them I was the best dancer when I was your age."

I swallowed. Then I put my mouth on the microphone. "When Ms. Homeyer was our age, she used to dance on the weekends."

Skeeter gripped the pew in front of him. I should not be doing this. I should not be doing this.

Ms. Dead Homeyer kept going.

"Tell them I used to be beautiful. I got my hair done in fancy salons, and my dad was the mayor and everyone used to want to be with me."

I took a breath and said it, "She used to be beautiful. She got her hair done in salons, and her dad was the mayor and everyone wanted to be with her."

Tony yelled, "Yeah right!"

Laughing now.

Gabby was staring straight at me.

Ms. Dead Homeyer whispered some more. "Tell them one time, I was dancing at Saltair Dance Club and I met the love of my life named Ed, and he was quite a looker."

I knew. I knew I could not say that. I knew I could not say anything I was saying but at the same time, I had no choice. A dead lady was talking to me.

My voice rang in the microphone, the feedback coming on as I told them about Ed.

"Ed was tall, had dark hair, wore wing-tip shoes and he said, 'Hey, I'm Ed.' And Ms. Homeyer said, 'I'm Carla,' and he said, 'Carla, how about you and me dance for the rest of our lives.'"

Suddenly no one was giggling or whispering. They were all fixed on me, and this was a huge mistake. If they made fun of me before, they were really going to go for it now.

125

But Ms. Homeyer bounced on her toes.

"See? They didn't know that. No one here knew that. No one here knew me. Tell them he thought I was pretty and intelligent and we would laugh for hours."

She was talking fast, her voice light.

My heart pounded and I told them. I told them stories about the two of them. The time they went bowling and Ed lost his shirt in a bet. I told them about when they used to go to the drive-in and kiss for hours. "Hours and hours," she said.

I told them about the day they got married. She wore a white mermaid dress with pearl flowers hand stitched into the fabric, and he wore his best army clothes, and it was magical with chocolate cake and a twenty-five-piece brass band.

I told them everything about her love, Ed.

As I spoke, people listened. They laughed at places and they gasped at places and when there was a wedding, I felt like I was there and so was everyone else. Ms. Dead Homeyer as a young beautiful girl. Her hair in real curls. Her dress swirling and her husband, Ed. I could see her and she was laughing and she was happy.

Then she said, "Tell them Ed died."

I looked at her.

"Look forward," she said. "Don't look at me."

I looked forward and she said, "Tell them . . ." she stopped, her voice catching. Then she said, "Tell them he was hit by a truck when we were newlyweds."

My hands started to shake.

"Go on," she said.

"Uh, he died," I said. "He died. Her husband, Ed, died."

A girl in the back said, "What?"

"By a truck," Ms. Dead Homeyer said. "Tell them it was an Associated Foods truck."

"He got hit by an Associated Foods truck."

Tony laughed out loud. His voice echoing and bouncing against the minty green walls.

Ms. Dead Homeyer had tears in her eyes.

Tony said, "This is so weird. Emmy is a freak."

Now Ms. Dead Homeyer was crying. Wiped her nose on her sleeve.

She sat down on the carpet and I wanted to say, Get up. Please get up and tell me what to say but she put her dead head in her hands.

I looked out and the spell was broken. People were laughing and whispering and the lady with the yellow hair and the muumuu gave me a thumbs-up, which made me feel even worse.

• 28 •

When I was ten I had a dream I was floating in the ocean.
The sun was overhead and there was no one around and
I felt good.

Light.

I wasn't scared. I didn't feel lonely.

Then I saw a shark.

The shark came up to me and started to circle.

I watched its fin go around and around and around.

I still wasn't scared.

I remember that well.

I wasn't scared. I was almost happy.

And then it bit my leg off.

Just like that. He swam right up and bit it off.

I watched him do it and he watched me watch him do it, and after he did it, he said, "You taste disgusting."

Then he swam away.

Ever since then I have the dream again.

And again.

And again.

And again.

"You taste disgusting."

Then he swims away.

• 29 •

When we got on the bus to go home from Ms. Dead Homeyer's funeral, Skeeter said, "That was weird."

My whole body was tingling. On fire. I felt confused and tired and jumpy.

"Yeah," I said. "It was weird."

I sat down next to the window again and tried to settle my nerves.

He sat next to me and said, "Really, why did you say all that? How did you know that stuff? I didn't even know Ms. Homeyer was married."

"I didn't know either," I said.

"Was it true?"

I shrugged.

I didn't want to think about it. Not right then, so I looked out the window and waited for him to begin talking about something else.

Waited. And waited.

It took him a while but then he started.

The bus drove slowly through town and Skeeter's voice was actually nice, like a warm blanket. We passed the spot where the kid had been holding the Dr. Ted Farnsworth sign.

That was tomorrow. Tomorrow a hundred people were going to sit through his seminar and tomorrow a hundred people were going to be convinced you could talk to dead people.

Like Kim.

People who were dying were going to think they weren't going to be dead dead. They were going to think they could still talk to their friends.

I used to think it was a lie.

But . . .

I was wrong.

You could talk to dead people, just not the ones you wanted.

I put my hand in my bag and touched Dr. Ted Farnsworth's book. What did it mean? Why was this happening?

When we got to our stop, Skeeter said, "Do you want me to walk you home?"

I looked at him.

After Kim died, I was alone. And then the first day of ninth grade, he was in five of my classes. Five. Skeeter and his headphones and his stories. I'd known him forever but never really thought about him or noticed him. Now we ate lunch together and sat together and did nothing together. I wondered when he'd start hanging out with other people and leave me behind like Kim did.

Every day I thought it might happen but so far I'd been lucky.

I sort of did want him to walk me home.

"It's okay," I said.

"Are you sure?" he said.

And I said, "Yeah. It's okay."

"Are you really sure?" he said.

"I'll be okay," I said.

He nodded.

Then I said, "I might get murdered."

"What?"

"Nothing."

"No. What did you say?"

"Nothing." I tucked my hair behind my ear because I'm a weirdo.

"Okay," he said.

"Okay," I said.

And that was it.

30

Some people should never die. They should wear bikinis and tell their chubby friends that they're pretty.

They should go on dates and eat strawberries and get into college. They should become doctors and write books and go on *The Bachelor*, which is a really good show. They should get married and have babies and laugh. All day long.

Kim could laugh all day long.

Kim was serious about Dr. Ted Farnsworth though, and when Kim was serious, it was hard to stop her.

It was in a few months but she was planning everything. Everything.

She rifled through my closet. "What do you wear to dead people visitation conventions?" she asked. She held up a silk blouse my mom had gotten me from Spain that was three sizes too big. "This?"

"We don't have to decide right now, do we?"

She pulled out another one. "You should wear this."

The shirt was one of my favorites from H&M. It was loose and had ruffles down the front and blue flowers that matched my eyes. The best part of me.

I wore the shirt on special occasions like talent shows.

"I'm not wearing that," I said.

"Why not?"

"Because I'm not going," I said. "I'm really not going. I hate the strip."

And this was true. I hated hated hated going to the strip. We never went anyway but the few times I did, I felt grimy and gross.

She put the shirt on the bed. "You're going," she said, not looking at me. "Besides, it's at Circus Circus. Not the strip."

"Circus Circus is on the strip."

"The old part of the strip," she said, which was not a

good point. The old part was just as bad as the new part. Worse.

My stomach started to ache. She turned back to the closet. "I want to pick out what we would wear in case we do go. I think we should be prepared," she said.

I watched Mickey Mouse's face on the back of her T-shirt.

It was November. The presentation was in February. Why was she so determined?

"It costs a lot," I said.

"I'll pay for it."

"You don't have any money."

"I'll figure it out."

I sat as she pulled out three more shirts.

We didn't talk about it after that and I hoped she'd forgotten. Or decided it was a dumb idea.

But then one day she called me and said it's all set up.

"What's all set up?"

"Dr. Ted Farnsworth convention on Saturday."

"Saturday? Is it this Saturday?"

"Yes, Emmy. I wrote it on your calendar."

I looked. February 12th, Dr. Ted Farnsworth.

Crap.

"We aren't really doing that are we?"

"Yes. We are."

I did not want to go. I did not want to go.

"How are we getting there?" I said.

Circus Circus was at least thirty minutes away.

"I got Perry to say he would take us," she said.

"Perry?"

Perry lived in Kim's crappy apartment complex. He was a senior at Cimarron, and he had his front tooth knocked out in a fight.

"You asked Perry?"

"He said it would be fine."

"Of course he said it would be fine, Kim. He loves you."

She laughed. "Whatever. We'll pick you up at nine. He said he'd take us right up to the door so you don't have to walk around on the strip."

I tried to think. Think. She had asked Perry to take us. He was going to take us right up to the door. She wasn't joking.

I took a breath. Then I asked, "Is Gabby going?"

She paused for a second and my heart sank.

Then she said, "Why would Gabby go?"

Relief poured through my body.

"I don't know," I said. "I just thought, you know. You might want Gabby to go."

"I don't want her to go, Emmy. I want you to go."

I stared at the poster of cats on my wall. She wanted me. Everything was confusing and messed up and I sat there.

"Will you go?" she said. "It'll be funny."

I tried to figure out if this was the right thing to do.

"Are you telling your mom?" I asked.

"Are you kidding? No way. And you can't tell yours."

"What am I supposed to say?"

"Tell her we're going to the library."

"Okay," I said.

She breathed into the phone and then she said, "Thank you, Emmers. Thank you so much."

31

One time, in a documentary, a lady talked about how peaceful it was to die.

She was surrounded by love and safety. Almost like a baby in the womb.

"Do you believe that?" Kim said.

"I don't know," I said.

My mom is an atheist. She thinks that when you die, you go to the ground and become part of the earth.

"It's actually quite beautiful," Mom said once.

Joe said, "You think it's beautiful to turn into dirt?"

She threw a piece of popcorn at him.

My dad, I don't know what he believes. His parents died in a car crash on their way to buy milk. Dad was eighteen.

He never talks about it.

Mom's parents weren't dead.

They lived in Phoenix in a condo development with other old people and golfed four times a week.

I stared in my bedroom mirror and tried not to care.

Not care about any of it.

About my boring brown hair

About my freckle face.

About my fat.

Who cares.

Who cares.

Who cares.

I was the type of person who should die. Not someone like Kim.

• 32 •

Sometimes, when you go home from a funeral of a dead science teacher and she made you tell her life story, it makes you exhausted. My bones ached and it felt like I hadn't slept in days.

I walked in the dark, the streetlamps still off, and as I got near my house, I heard something.

It was far away, and faint.

Like humming.

The houses on the street were mostly dark. Pushed together in a row, like LEGOS.

As I got closer, it got louder.

Someone was singing a song.

Low. Quiet.

Two houses away from mine I recognized it. "We Are Young" by Fun.

My heart pounded. On the rare times we were at Kim's apartment, we had a tradition where we'd scream that song. Jump on her bed and hit the ceiling with our fists and Trish would always, always, without fail come yell at us.

We'd stop and Kim would say, "Sorry, Mom."

And I'd say, "Sorry, Trish."

She'd say, "My hell."

Then she'd turn and slam the door.

We'd wait three minutes. Three minutes on Kim's Hello Kitty clock, then we'd turn it back on again. Louder.

Right then, though, in the darkness, the song was melodic. Not loud. Not screaming. It was soft and floating. A female's voice.

My heart thumped.

I stopped walking.

"Kim," I whispered.

The palms on the trees swayed in the wind, bringing the sounds loud and then soft like the ocean. It made it difficult to tell where it was coming from.

"Kim?" I said a little louder.

I turned around. Houses. Astroturf. A piece of paper dancing along the road.

I looked for a light from the sky. Or a feeling. Dr. Ted Farnsworth said it could be a feeling at first and then get stronger.

But there was nothing. Chills ran up my back.

I started walking again and the song got louder.

When I was in front of my house, it was distinct.

Tonight. We are young. So let's set the world on fire.

My heart pounded harder now.

I looked across the road and she was sitting there. On the curb. She was sitting there hunched over.

Singing Fun.

Ms. Dead Homeyer. Again.

In person, Dr. Ted Farnsworth was slimmer but much older than his picture. He had sweaty armpits, and when he spoke, he smacked his lips. Loud echoing smacks that reverberated in the stale conference room at Circus Circus.

Perry and Kim had shown up right on time, and Mom said, "Who is that with Kim?"

I grabbed my bag and started for the door. "Emmy. Who is that?"

"It's her neighbor. We're going to the library."

Then I ran out before she could say anything. I knew she'd be worried about Perry because his goatee was disgusting and he had a tattoo of a dragon on his neck. She also didn't approve of large trucks.

When I got in Perry said, "Hi, Emmy."

And I said, "Hi, Perry."

And Kim said, "I'm excited."

Her hair wasn't in a ponytail and she'd put on mascara. "I think it's going to be so cool," she said.

I nodded. "Yeah. It should be cool."

Perry said, "What is it you're going to again?"

Kim put her finger in his ear and he swerved.

"What the crap, Kim."

She laughed and turned up the music and soon we were at Circus Circus.

There are many casinos in Las Vegas. Some of them are glittering and gold and have long stretch limos in the front. Some of them have magical fountains and tigers with ladies in Princess Leia costumes. And some of them are Circus Circus.

We walked through the hallways. I'd been here once to a birthday party when I was nine. It was dark and heavy and screaming from the rides and the carnival area where the girl had had her birthday cake and it felt like a cave with old people trying to get us to give them money so we could throw beanbags at milk cans.

"I wonder why he's having his seminar here," I said.

Kim was walking fast. Her bag bouncing on her back as she went. I almost had to run to catch up. "What?"

"Why is it here?" I said again. "If Dr. Ted Farnsworth is such a big deal, if he's famous and important and people from all over the world come to see him, why would he rent a room in the back of Circus Circus?"

Why is it here?

Kim had a map of the casino in her hand and she said, "This place is a maze. I can't find Meeting Room A," ignoring my question.

The whole place felt stale.

It took us five more minutes and three workers' instructions to finally get there.

There was a big sign with the same picture from his bio.

WELCOME, BELIEVERS!

TALKING BEYOND

BY DR. TED FARNSWORTH!!!

WORLD CLASS MEDIUM AND MENTOR

"This is it," she said. "This is it!" And she walked right in like we belonged in a place like Meeting Room A.

I stood in the hall and watched her go inside. We had

done so many things together and I always trusted her. I always trusted her that it would turn out okay.

But this time it felt different.

I stood in the hall and she came back out, "Come on," she whispered. "It's starting."

I took a breath and followed her in.

Kim and I sat in the back, and Meeting Room A of Circus Circus was full of almost-dead people. Oxygen machines. Walkers. Somebody with a helmet on which I didn't know what that meant.

Kim handed me a notebook.

"What's this?" I said.

"Paper."

"Why?"

"So we can take notes, duh."

She had a purple pen for me and a turquoise one for her. She also gave me a water bottle. She was prepared.

A lady with blue hair turned around and smiled at us. We smiled back.

Then the lights went out and some tiny stars appeared. Like we were at a laser show.

"WELCOME," a voice said from the speakers in the

back of the room. "WELCOME, BROTHERS AND SISTERS."

Some strange music started playing.

"What is happening," I whispered.

"Shhhhh."

Soon the music was replaced with "Forever Young."

"Are you kidding me?"

Kim elbowed me.

Finally a lady with a tight black dress on and huge blond hair ran up onstage and started clapping her hands over her head.

"WELCOME, MY BROTHERS AND SISTERS!!!!!! THIS IS THE BEST DAY OF THE REST OF YOUR ETERNAL LIVES."

Old people started clapping with her. Kim started clapping. I sunk in my seat.

A spotlight was swinging from wall to wall.

"INTRODUCING THE INCREDIBLE, THE BEAUTIFUL, THE WONDERFUL DOCTOR TED FARNSWORTH!!!!!!!!!!!!!!!!!!!!"

The spotlight swerved to a dented door in the corner. The music got lower and we waited for the incredible, the beautiful, the wonderful Dr. Ted Farnsworth.

We waited.

And we waited.

The lady with the blond hair said, "He's coming. He's on his way."

We waited.

And then, when people were starting to get restless and a large man with a shiny head said, "I want my money back," right then, Dr. Ted Farnsworth burst through the door.

He was wearing a green golf shirt and a blazer. His hair was greasy, which I whispered to Kim, "He looks like Leo."

She hit me. Leo lived in Kim's apartment complex and bought Kim whipped cream for her birthday. He was disgusting. "Shh," she said.

Dr. Ted Farnsworth ran up to the stage.

"HELLO, MY FRIENDS!!!!!" He yelled into the microphone.

People clapped.

"THE THINGS YOU LEARN TODAY WILL TRANSFORM THE WAY YOU LOOK AT LIFE, DEATH, AND YOURSELF."

The spotlight shone on a white screen. No picture came up.

"WHAT DO YOU SEE?" he asked.

Someone yelled, "Nothing."

Someone else yelled, "White."

A third person said, "It's broken."

Dr. Ted Farnsworth walked into the spotlight and said, "You're all right and you're all wrong.

"WHAT YOU SEE HERE IS AN ILLUSION. WE ALL HAVE OUR PERCEPTIONS OF THIS BLANK WALL, BUT WHAT YOU ARE REALLY SEEING IS . . ."

He waited.

This was idiotic but Kim was on the edge of her seat.

He started talking again, "What you're seeing, people, IS POSSIBILITY! HOPE! DEATH!"

It was a blank screen.

Then an actual PowerPoint showed up.

According to Dr. Ted, that first year was when the most visitations happened.

"Usually on important dates," Dr. Ted said.

Dr. Ted said, "Birthdays, anniversaries, graduations, all those days are prime time for you to come back and tell your family you are still with them. You still love them. You're still a part of their lives."

A lady behind me burped.

"Kim," I whispered, "can we go?"

"Shh," she said, digging her fingers into my thigh. "Listen," she said.

Dr. Ted pointed to a slide on the screen. "The most important date, the date when you are almost guaranteed special time with your loved ones . . . if they are prepared, that is . . . is the anniversary of your death. Not only the anniversary, but the minute."

PICTURE OF A STOPWATCH

"The exact minute the body and spirit separated. That minute is the minute you will, with 99.99 percent guarantee or your money back, that minute you will feel contact from your loved one. The veil is thin, my friends, the veil is thin."

Kim scribbled on her notebook.

I felt sick to my stomach.

34

A light went on in my house.

My dad was most likely working late, and Joe was probably out with his butthead friends, but Mom would be waiting. Reading a self-help book and waiting.

She was always waiting for me.

"Sit down," Ms. Dead Homeyer said.

So I sat down.

She started humming again.

This time it was "We Don't Need No Education" by Pink
Floyd.

I scooted farther away from her. She stopped humming
and looked at me. "You're a funny girl," she said.

I'm a funny girl? Me?

Then she said, "And this is a big weekend, isn't it?"

My heart started thumping again. How did she know that? Why was she here? Did she see Kim?

She was playing with her shoelace and she said, "It's not what people think. You know what I mean?"

I had no idea what she meant. I just wanted her to tell me if Kim was coming. "I don't know what you mean," I said.

She smiled. "I think you do."

Then she stood up.

"I have to go."

"You have to go?" I said.

"Yes. I have to go. There will be others."

"Others?"

Now my heart was really thumping. She walked over and squatted down in close to my face and said, "Emmy? Don't let anyone forget about Ed, okay?"

"What?"

But she was gone.

35

Ms. Dead Homeyer died suddenly, but Kim was dying before she was even born.

She had pulmonary atresia.

That meant the right valve into her heart didn't work like it was supposed to. Usually this could be fixed. But then she had a lot of other complications with other parts of her heart. Things leaking, not pumping enough, and on and on.

Trish and my mom worked at Denny's when they were both pregnant with us. Then my dad finished law school and my mom quit Denny's and Trish got into some trouble at a casino and had to work overtime.

My mom was in the hospital room when Kim was born, holding Trish's hand.

"It was so scary," Mom would say.

"What do you mean?"

Mom brushed my hair at night and sometimes I'd ask her about it even though I'd heard the story a hundred times. "They had to do open heart surgery right away. And she was just a teeny tiny baby."

The bristles of the brush felt good against my scalp.

"The doctors didn't think she would make it through the night. Her poor little body with all the tubes and the wires and the pumps."

Kim who talked me into putting all the lawn chairs in the pool to see if we could walk across the water. Kim who made a macaroni salad statue for the science fair. Kim who was determined to one day own her own hot-dog truck.

Mom stopped talking.

"What happened then?" I asked.

She sighed. "Then, Trish was crying and I was crying. And a man walked into her room."

This was my favorite part.

"He just walked in like he belonged there. They don't let you do that nowadays," she said. "There's security."

"What did he look like," I asked. Like I asked every time.

"He was short. He was round. He was bald and he had a bouquet of balloons. He handed the balloons to Trish.

"'What's this for?' Trish said, her eyes red.

"He said, 'It's a delivery. For you and your baby.'"

Mom started braiding my hair then.

"And what did the card say," I asked.

It said, "Here's to many years of joy!!!!"

Mom stopped braiding. Pulled my hair out of the braid with her fingers and smoothed it down.

"What happened then?"

Mom put her arms around me. "Then," she said, "then your best friend showed she was a fighter."

I smiled. Kim was a fighter. She'd had surgery after surgery her whole life and she was still here.

Fine.

Perfect.

Fine.

36

After Ms. Dead Homeyer left my neighborhood and I went
inside and sat on my bed.

My mom came in.

She sat by me and I could tell she wanted to have a talk.

I did not want to have a talk. I don't like to have talks.

I said, "Hi."

She said, "Where have you been?"

I said what I always say, "The library."

She said, "You were at the library?"

I said, "Yes."

She said . . .

I said . . .

She said . . .

I said . . .

She said, "I was worried about you. It's late."

I said, "Oh."

She said, "I think I'm done letting you go off places by yourself."

I looked at her. "You are?"

She said, "I worry so much."

I said, "I'm okay."

She said, "I don't know."

Then I said, "I'm okay."

And she said, "I called Dad. He's going to pick up a pizza on his way home."

I said, "Oh."

Then she said, "Emmy. Please tell me what's going on."

I nodded. I could feel tears coming on. Like they were right there, right on the edge, and I wanted to let them come out.

But I didn't.

Instead I said, "I'm fine."

She looked at me and I looked at my hands.

Ms. Dead Homeyer said there'd be more. I had to hold it together.

Mom rubbed my back.

"Will you come down when Dad gets here?"

I shrugged. "I'm really tired."

She was watching me. I could feel her watching me and I wished everything were different. I never knew what to say to her anymore. What to say to anyone anymore.

"Okay," she said.

"Okay," I said.

She left.

37

My mom gave me a lecture once.

I had to get a training bra.

She took me to Macy's and bought me a bra in a box that said, My First Bra.

"Mom. I don't need this."

"You do need this."

"Why doesn't Kim have to get one?"

Mom had dropped Kim off at her apartment before we came shopping. Usually Kim went with us every-where but Mom had said, "Kimmer. Emmy and I have some business we have to attend to in private."

Kim had given me a look and I had no idea.

"Okay, Linda," Kim said. "Where are you going?"

"It's a secret."

"From me?"

"Yep."

"What's going on?" I said.

Mom pulled into the lot of Kim's apartment. "You can come over tonight if you want."

Kim looked hurt.

"Can I just go wherever you're going and sit in the car?"

"Nope," Mom said. "I'm sorry."

Mom never did this. Ever.

So we bought a bra and in the car I said, "Why couldn't Kim come?"

Mom started humming and I said, "Mom?"

"Mom?

"Mom?"

And finally, "Mom, why couldn't Kim come?"

She slowed at a stoplight and then she looked at me. "Emmy. You and Kim are different."

I felt myself get hot and I didn't even know why.

She kept going. "I know this is hard to hear but things are going to change. You have different bodies. You have different personalities. You'll be starting high school soon.

"You can't do everything together forever, Emmy."

I sat.

We couldn't do everything together forever.

Or could we?

When school started, I realized Mom was right. Things were changing.

I felt like I was living two different lives. The one where it was just me and Kim and we talked about the afterlife and Dr. Ted Farnsworth and chocolate fountains, and the one where Gabby was around and Kim was louder than usual and went to the mall all the time and wore eye shadow.

Maybe we wouldn't do everything together.

There was a passage in those books. I don't remember which, but not Dr. Ted Farnsworth's. One book said, You are never alone.

Is that true?

38.

I sat for awhile.

Then I went to my computer and typed in SALTAIR DANCE CLUB.

Immediately there were 68,900,678 results.

The first one, a history of Saltair, said this:

> Located on the southern shore of Utah's Great
> Salt Lake, The Saltair Pavilion opened its doors for
> business in 1893. The girth of the resort rested
> on over 2,000 pylons, driven into the bed along
> the lakeshore. Many of the original posts can still

be seen today, over a hundred years after the resort's initial construction.

The Coney Island of the west, couples could visit Saltair by taking a short train ride and dance the night away without becoming victims of indecorous rumors.

I stared at it. There was a Saltair.

You could dance there and not become "victims of indecorous rumors."

Ms. Homeyer met her husband there.

He was perfect.

She was pretty.

It was real. This was real.

I googled his name, Ed Homeyer.

This one was harder. Ed Homeyer in Culver City wants to be your real estate agent.

Ed Homeyer, ppl directory.

Ed Homeyer, editor in chief of *Poughkeepsie Daily News*.

And then I saw it. Ed Homeyer. Carla Homeyer. Salt Lake City. Ancestry.com

I stared at it.

Ed Homeyer was a real person which meant everything that was happening was real.

I'd seen a ghost.

This was real.

Dad came in my room then. He was in his suit and he looked tired.

He said, "Hey."

I said, "Hey," and tried to be calm.

"What you looking at?"

I clicked the screen closed.

"You okay?"

"Yep."

He kept looking at me, so I picked up a flyer from school that said, HOW MANY POUNDS OF FOOD WILL YOU DONATE? PALO VERDE FOOD DRIVE.

"What's that?" he said.

"Food drive."

"Oh," he said. Then he said, "I got chicken alfredo pizza. It's downstairs."

I said, "Is there bacon?"

He said, "No. I forgot the bacon."

I said, "That's okay."

He closed the blinds.

I wished he hadn't closed the blinds.

He said, "Emmy. What's going on?"

I said, "Nothing."

He said, "Nothing?"

I said, "Yeah. Nothing."

He said, "Your room is pretty bad."

I said, "Yeah."

He said, "It seems like maybe you should clean it up some-time."

I said, "Yeah."

He said, "It's really messy."

I said, "Yeah."

He said . . .

I said . . .

He said . . .

I said . . .

He said, "Okay. I'm going to go back downstairs."

I said, "Okay."

He said, "Your mom and I are going to watch a movie. You should come down."

I said, "No thanks."

He sighed and I thought maybe he'd try to talk to me too. Like Mom.

But instead he just turned and left.

And I was relieved.

166

39

It didn't work on my birthday. Kim didn't appear and I'd done everything right. So then I tried her birthday— only two months after mine. September.

I reread the chapter on visitations and special occasions.

I got the cupcakes.

I got the Fresca.

I got *Ladyhawke*.

I got the Snickers, Skittles, and this time peanut butter M&M's because if it didn't work again, I thought I should be left with candy I wanted to eat rather than stuff myself with ones I didn't really like.

It was the third week of ninth grade.

I walked to the school bus stop; Gabby was there. Skeeter. Other kids from our neighborhood.

I crossed the street and kept walking.

"Hey," Gabby yelled as I passed.

I kept going. What did she want? Why would she try to talk to me now? Today? She hadn't even glanced at me for weeks. Months.

"Hey. Emmy!"

I turned to look and they were all staring at me.

"Where are you going?" Gabby said.

I felt bile coming up my throat. I should have waited. I should have walked out my door and sat in the bushes until the school bus was gone. One time I sat in my bushes for three hours while I was waiting to scare Joe after one of his dates. I can hold very still.

I should have sat in the bushes.

I stopped on the sidewalk and tried to decide what to do. The Red Rock bus stop was a mile away.

I looked over at them.

Gabby had her hand on her hip like usual. Skeeter was standing near her, also watching me.

I turned and kept walking. Fast. The school bus passed me, and I heard Gabby yell something but I didn't look back.

When I turned the corner I had to stop and catch my breath.

Catch my breath.

Catch my breath.

Then I heard someone and if it was Gabby I didn't know what I was going to say. But then he came around the corner and it was Skeeter.

"Where are you going?" He was breathing hard and I was sort of happy to see him. I don't know why.

"You're going to miss the bus," I said.

"I don't care."

He had sweat dripping down his face, and I said, "Did everyone see you run after me?"

He said, "I don't care."

I said, "I'm not doing anything fun." And he said, "I don't care."

✳ ✳ ✳

So me and Skeeter sat at our rock on Kim's birthday.

We ate the Snickers bars and I told him—he was the first person I told, the only person I told—about Kim. About how I was supposed to meet her here. I thought he would laugh but instead he said, "How is she going to come? Like from the clouds?"

"I don't know," I said. "It doesn't say how, or anything. It just says if you do the right preparation, the veil will thin and she'll come here."

"Like sit here?"

"I don't know."

He looked up at the sky. "Did you do the right preparation?"

I shrugged. "I tried."

He nodded. "I'm sure you did."

We ate some more Snickers and sat.

It felt good to have someone with me. To not be alone.

"My brother totaled his truck," he told me. "He had to go to the ER."

"Oh," I said.

Then I said, "Joe and his girlfriend got caught making out in my dad's car."

"Which one?"

"The Mustang."

He laughed.

We talked about whether Snickers or Reese's Peanut Butter Cups were better. He told me he hated washing dishes at his dad's Little Caesars and I said I always felt bad he had to work there and he explained Guns N' Roses is actually a really good band.

"They just scream."

"They don't scream," he said. And then he started singing "Sweet Child O' Mine."

So we sat there all day long while everyone else was in school.

We sat there all day long and waited for Kim.

Every hour on the hour I made him be quiet and I sat with my legs crossed and my eyes closed and he said, "Should I hum something."

"Shhh."

"Should I close my eyes?"

I looked at him. "Uh. Yeah."

He closed his eyes.

And every hour on the hour, she didn't come.

• 40 •

I sat on my bed and watched outside for more dead people.

Or for Kim.

I was waiting for Kim.

I put on my ratty nightgown. Kim had the same one. I put it on and shoved Mom's sequin dress under my bed. Then I sat.

The streetlight that Ms. Dead Homeyer used to be sitting under stayed the same.

All night long.

No Kim.

No other ghosts.

No nothing.

By five in the morning, my legs were aching and my head hurt.

I wrapped myself in an old Disney Princess blanket, stepped into my bunny slippers, and went and sat on the front porch to watch the sunrise.

There was a bird.

Another bird.

The sky was gray and no one was out except for an old lady with a dog that barked at me, and the lady said shut up, and three more birds.

Today is the day my best friend died.

Today is the day my best friend died.

Today is the day my best friend died.

The sky slowly turned to pink with purples and blues and oranges.

It seemed like it shouldn't be so beautiful.

I put in my earbuds and turned on Dr. Ted Farnsworth's CDs that I'd downloaded. I hadn't listened to them for months. I carried his book in my bag, just in case. But I hardly ever listened to him. His voice made me itch.

But now I thought I should. I should try harder.

I closed my eyes.

You must be present during the visitation. You must concentrate. They want to be with you. They want to visit you. They yearn for it. You are the one stopping it. YOU.

I tried to concentrate. I tried to be present. I tried to let her come.

Please let her come.

Please let her come.

Please let her come.

She wants to come.

You must believe. Believe it. Know it. Be it.

Believe it. Know it. Be it.

Believe it. Know it. Be it.

I whispered the words, trying to fill myself with pure thoughts.

Waterfalls.

Mountains.

Rainbows.

Then I heard something.

I turned off the iPod, goose bumps all over my body. I looked around.

There was nothing.

I stood up and looked down the street.

Nothing.

I looked the other way.

Nothing.

I looked up in the sky.

Nothing.

I tried again.

Let yourself blend into the environment. Integrate yourself with the whole. Forget the past and the future and focus on the now. Only then will the veil become thin enough for someone to enter.

I turned it off.

Blend into the environment.

Be part of the whole.

Focus on now.

Now.

The morning.

The pink sky.

The birds.

The sound started up again.

My heart fluttered.

I didn't open my eyes this time, instead I focused on the now, and I kept listening to his voice. *Be your real you. Be your authentic self. Listen to the universe and the universe will listen to you.*

I listened to the universe. I turned off the voice and I listened to the universe.

And the universe said, "Hey."

In a boy voice. It said, hey.

I opened my eyes.

Joe was standing on the porch.

"Hey," he said.

I sighed.

• 41 •

Sometimes I think about how I'm going to die.

There are so many ways.

You can die from carpet-cleaning fumes.

You can die from drinking too much carrot juice.

You can die from laughing.

One time on this show *1000 WAYS TO DIE*, which is also a really good show, one time a girl got killed tying her shoe.

"That would never happen," Joe said.

"What? These are all true stories," Kim said.

"They are not." Joe flopped on the couch and I had to turn it up.

"You can only watch with us if you don't make dumb comments."

Joe said, "Really? You have to make dumb comments when you watch something this idiotic."

"It's the rule," Kim said.

The next guy on the show died by eating too many Egg McMuffins.

"That is so gross," Kim said.

"It is really gross," I said.

Joe said, "Shhhhh." And then we watched the rest of the episode.

• 42 •

Joe sat on the bench next to me.

We sat there.

And sat there.

And sat there.

"What are you doing up so early?" I finally said.

He looked bad. His eyes bloodshot, his freckles redder than usual.

"I couldn't sleep," he said.

I pulled my blanket tighter. "Why not?"

He looked at me. "What do you mean, why not?"

"I mean why not?"

"Em, I know what day it is."

He knew what day it was. Sometimes I felt like I was the only one. The only one who remembered anything. But then that was stupid. Joe loved her, too. Everyone loved her.

We sat for a while again. Then he said, "I wish I hadn't bet on that kid."

I looked at him. "What?"

"That kid," he said.

"Oh," I said. "Yeah."

A few months before Kim died, a kid had been killed on the New York-New York Roller Coaster. A boy from Joe's grade.

Mom had said, "Did you know him, Joe?"

And Joe stuffed his bagel in his mouth.

Kim looked at me. I looked at her. He was being weird.

"Joe." Mom held up the news article. "Do you know this kid? He fell out of the roller coaster?"

"He fell out?" I said.

"Yeah," Mom said. "It says he somehow didn't have the restraint on properly, and it came loose during part of the ride."

Kim turned white and I had to put down my milk.

Joe on the other hand was still shoving bagels in his mouth.

"You didn't know him?" Mom said.

"No," he said, crumbs blowing all over.

Mom started reading out loud, "'Baylor Frederick Hicks died in a tragic accident on the New York-New York Roller Coaster. Baylor was a sophomore at Palo Verde High and just recently placed in the district science fair with his hydraulics system. The ride will be shut down for the next few days to make sure the blah blah blah.'"

"That's strange," Dad said.

"Yeah," Kim said, "that's really strange. The restraints are high tech. They push them down when you get on."

Joe turned red and in went another bagel.

"Family of Baylor are devastated. He was an amazing young man. Everyone who knew him loved him. Graveside services will be announced soon."

After breakfast, we followed Joe upstairs.

"Who was that kid?" Kim said.

Joe never acted like this.

He kept walking. Into his room and tried to shut the door.

"What are you doing?" Kim said, and pushed in anyway.

Joe sat at his desk and Kim sat on his desk, knocking over pencils and papers, which you don't do in Joe's room, and I stood in the doorway.

"I have stuff to do," Joe said.

"You did know him," Kim said.

She was mad. Kim could get mad at stuff and you could hear it in her voice.

Joe said, "Whatever. He was just a kid from my grade."

Kim stared at him. "You knew him."

"Sort of."

"Why didn't you tell Mom?" I said.

He shrugged. "I don't feel like talking about it." He turned on his computer.

"I'm not going anywhere," Kim said. "I want to know what happened."

Joe clicked on ESPN sports.

We waited.

"Joe," Kim said, "I'm not leaving."

I swallowed.

Finally Joe turned around, his face now more than red.

"I didn't know him," Joe said. "I really didn't. But every-one was talking about how he was going to try to ride part of the roller coaster without a restraint. He was going to do the upside down part without the harness and then pull it back down."

"What?"

Joe shook his head. "I don't know. He had it all worked

out. He said he could do it. That the laws of physics would hold him in."

"What?"

"He said that. He was bragging about it and someone said then do it and he said he would. Then it got to be this thing. People were betting."

"People were betting?"

A bead of sweat formed on Joe's forehead. "The kid was a loser," Joe said, and I felt like I'd been punched.

I'd never heard Joe talk like that about anyone. Did he say things like that all the time? Did he think I was a loser?

He kept going. "He was the one who planned it, you know. He was the one who figured out how to release the restraint. It was his idea. He said on the upside part you wouldn't fall out."

I stared at Joe.

Kim said, "Did you bet on him?"

Joe wiped his face and turned back to the computer screen.

"Did you bet on him, Joe?" Kim said. Her voice rising.

He clicked on an article about steroids.

"Did you lose money or make money?"

Joe shook his head. Clicked on another article.

Kim stood up. "That's sick," she said. "That's really sick."

Joe's shoulders sagged and I stood there. Trying to figure out what to feel.

Now she was gone and we were sitting in the early morning hours of her death anniversary and he said, "I wish I hadn't bet on that kid."

And I said, "I wish you hadn't either."

And then my big brother started to cry.

• 43 •

I had never seen Joe cry.

Not when my grandma died.

Not when he got dumped by Amy Dudworthy.

Not even the time when he got cut from the basketball team in sixth grade.

But right then, the sun peeking over the hills, the sounds of the garbage truck making the early morning rounds, a new fresh day, and he was sitting next to me, not just crying, but sobbing.

I sat there and let him cry for a while I guess. I actually don't know what I was doing. I just felt sad.

So I did one thing. I put my hand on his shoulder.

He stopped crying and looked at me, his face all streaked with tears. And I said, "What?"

And he said, "What are you doing?"

And I said, "Trying to help?"

"What?"

"I'm helping you," I said.

"You're helping me?"

So then he started to laugh.

"Why are you laughing?" I said. It was pretty rude.

He laughed even harder.

Then I couldn't help it, I started to laugh.

And laugh and laugh and laugh.

Then my mom came out in her old lady housedress and said, "You two are going to wake up the whole neighborhood."

That's when we really lost it.

Five months after Kim died, my dad let me drive his
Saturn Sky.

I'm fifteen and don't know how to drive and I didn't
want to drive his Saturn Sky.

He said, "Come on, Em. It will make you feel alive."

My dad didn't know how to make people feel alive.

He worked too hard.

But sometimes he'd try.

Like once he took me to Wendy's at one in the morning to get a Frosty. And another time he checked me
and Kim out of school so we could see the premiere of
Tron at the IMAX.

He tried.

Then Kim died.

We were sitting in the Albertsons parking lot and his face was red with excitement. "We won't tell Joe. We won't tell your mother."

"Dad," I said. "I don't want to."

He said, "Just wait. Just wait. I promise you, Em."

He was so different from Mom who kept buying me Chicken Soup for the Soul books. *Chicken Soup for the Soul: Grieving and Recovery* or *Chicken Soup for the Soul: Tough Times for Teens* or *Chicken Soup for the Soul: Shaping the New You.*

He put the Sky in gear and peeled out of the parking lot. I gripped the armrest.

"Dad," I said.

"No talking," he said. "Don't talk. Just sit here and relax."

He turned up the music, Katy Perry, which was a weird choice.

I stared out the window and tried to think of things, like whether I should shave my head. He drove to a little two-lane road and stopped on the shoulder.

"You want to feel something, Emmy? You want to feel?"

Ugh.

"Not really," I said, but he didn't hear because he was getting out of the car. He got out and I got out. He gave me a high five as he passed me and then I sat in the driver's seat, and he said, "Go ahead," and I said, "Dad."

He smiled. "Do it."

"Dad, I really don't—"

He cut me off and said, "Do it."

And so I drove his Saturn Sky.

One mile.

My foot back and forth on the gas, on the brake, because why would he think I'd want to do this? My neck getting sweaty under the weight of my fat hair and any second I knew, I knew we were going to get hit by a semi.

One mile.

He had his hand on the dash the whole time.

"Why'd you stop?" he said when I pulled over and the car almost bounced off the road. "Why'd you stop?" But he was already getting out and I was already getting out.

• 45 •

Mom made us come inside and it was warm and it smelled like waffles.

"You made breakfast?" Joe said.

My mom usually ate her diet food and we ate cereal.

"Your dad did."

"Dad?" We both said.

My dad loved to golf on Saturdays. He believed in it. Like he believed in *Monday Night Football* and eating ribs on the Fourth of July.

Every Saturday he went with his same friends, to the same course, at the same time.

But not today.

Today he was in his pajamas in the kitchen, whistling and frying bacon, and when we walked in, he said, "Greetings, Earthlings."

My dad could be such a dork.

I sort of forgot about that. How he was a dork. It was like I was coming out of a coma.

Mom had set the table and there was chocolate milk and bananas and strawberries and a bowl full of Skittles, a plate of Snickers, and a small chocolate fountain.

"What's this?" Joe said.

I bit my lip.

Mom said, "Your dad and I just thought we'd have a special meal this morning."

Dad brought the food over and Mom started dishing things out, but then Dad said, "Can we say a prayer?"

We all froze.

Mom said, "What?"

He said it again, "Can we say a prayer?"

We'd never said a prayer before in our house. At least not as a family.

Mom set down the waffle plate.

Joe looked at me.

Then my dad folded his arms, so we all folded our arms.

Then he closed his eyes.

191

So we all closed our eyes.

Then my dad, who is a corporate lawyer and takes power naps, my dad, he said a prayer.

He said:

Dear God.

Hey.

Please take care of our Kimberly. Let her know
we love her and miss her.

I opened my eyes.

Mom was watching him.

I closed my eyes again.

Tell her we think about her every day.

Thank you for the food.

Amen.

"Amen," we all said.

And then we ate breakfast.

• 46 •

When your best friend dies, things happen.

    You lie under your bed.

    You plan spiritual visitations.

    You watch a lot of TV.

    You eat turkey burgers.

One time, I sat in my room and watched Gabby.

    She was outside and she was with a couple of girls and some boys pulled up.

    It was the same Jeep as before and she was laughing so loud.

She was so easy at it.

Easy peasy.

The middle of ninth grade and she had five thousand friends.

They were talking and the sun was going down and it looked like how it should. Like they were real people, hanging out and being normal.

Why couldn't I be normal?

Gabby looked up at me, she was saying something into the Jeep, and she looked up at me and I ducked down.

I sat on the carpet and sat there.

In three days it was going to be Gabby's birthday.

Kim thought we should do a visitation for Gabby at Forever 21.

"What?"

"Yeah," she said. "I want to scare everyone who shops there. I think it'd be hilarious."

I stared at her. I hated that we talked about this all the time, and I hated that she wanted to do Gabby's at Forever 21.

"What do you mean you want to scare everyone?" I said.

She looked at her toenails. "Like I want to appear and the lights will flicker and everyone will talk about the haunted Forever 21."

"Which one?" I asked.

"Meadows Mall, of course."

I tried to process this. It was true, if anywhere would be good to haunt, Forever 21 at Meadows Mall would be the place. But I didn't want to do it.

Dr. Farnsworth said visitations aren't scary. "It's not like you'd be haunting us," I said.

She laughed. "I know. I just want to try."

"Gabby doesn't even know about all this," I said.

"It'll be a surprise."

I sat there. Then I said it. I'd said it before and now I was saying it again.

"You're not going to die."

She lay down on the bed, her hair splayed out.

"I am going to die."

"You don't know that. What about Jenny?"

One lady, Jenny Biggs from Rhode Island, Jenny lived until she was fifty-four, and she had the same thing as Kim—even as bad as Kim. We had been sort of obsessed with Jenny in sixth grade when Kim's doctor told her about her. We'd e-mailed her and Jenny Biggs was really cool. She sent us pictures of her family and her dog and told Kim that she should dream big. Dream old!

Now Jenny Biggs was dead.

"Jenny Biggs is dead," Kim said.

"I know but she lived for a long time."

"Jenny Biggs is dead," she said again.

Then she looked at me. "I really want to appear at Forever 21."

· 47 ·

After breakfast I went up to my room.

    Dad said a prayer.

    To God.

    About Kim.

    Like God was real.

    And like Kim was real.

    More than dust.

I took out a notebook.

    How to see Kim:

    Be present.

Wear light clothes.

Do visualization exercises.

Get back to nature.

Believe.

BELIEVE!!!

· 48 ·

Anyone who wants to can talk to dead people but some people are better at it than others.

THEY HAVE THE NATURAL SENSE FOR IT, Dr. Ted Farnsworth said into the microphone. We'd been at the seminar for two and a half hours. We'd gone over which times were the best to contact the dead, where were the best places to do the contacting, and finally, who were the best candidates to do the dirty work—which people were the ideal conduits for a return to earth. YOU NEED TO PICK SOMEONE WHO KNOWS YOU BETTER THAN ANYONE ELSE. SOMEONE YOU TRUST. SOMEONE WHO FEELS

WITH BOTH THEIR HEART, a picture of a heart came on the screen, AND THEIR BRAIN, now a picture of a brain.

I sat there.

Kim poked me with her pencil.

"What?"

"That's you," she whispered.

"Kim, I can't."

She put her finger to her lips and pointed at him.

ALL THEY NEED TO DO IS BE PREPARED. BE OPEN TO IT. MAKE THEIR BODY AS CLEAN AS THEY CAN.

He was crazy. This was crazy.

He went on and on and Kim scribbled in the notebook the entire time. I had never seen her like this. She didn't take notes in school. Ever. She had a hard time paying attention in one class, let alone a three-hour lecture on spiritual preparation.

When it was over and music was pumping and old people were swarming Dr. Ted Farnsworth near the refreshment table, Kim said, "What did you think?"

"Uh," I said. "I don't know."

She said, "I think it was amazing."

"You did?"

"Yeah. Like what if it really worked. Didn't you think that video was awesome?"

He'd shown a video of a lady talking to her dead real estate agent about a property that she wanted to buy.

"I mean," I said, "it was a little weird."

But Kim wasn't listening to me anymore. She was standing up and looking over at the crowd around Dr. Ted Farnsworth.

"Come on," she said. "I want to meet him."

I sat in my room.

The plan was on the day she died, I should meet her at the spot.

On the rock.

The minute of her death.

The MINUTE OF VISITATION!! An entire chapter in Dr. Ted Farnsworth's book.

We didn't know when that minute would be.

"What if it's at like three in the morning?" Kim had asked me.

We were eating fries and I was not thinking about when she was going to die. At least I was trying not to.

I said, "What?"

And she said, "What if I die in the night?"

I shoved the fry in mouth. "I don't know," I said.

"What if we don't know the exact minute?"

"I don't know."

"You would have to camp out there."

"Camp out there?"

"Camp on the rock."

I stared at her. "You want me to camp out there?"

She picked up her shake and sipped it while I sat there. She wanted me to camp out on the rock.

"By myself?"

She shrugged. "I don't know."

I don't know.

Luckily, Kim did not die in the middle of the night.

She died at 5:48 in the evening, during a hot spell.

One of the worst in Vegas history.

A hot spell where when you walked outside you felt like you were in hell. Like you were burning to the ground and soon would be a pile of ash and bones.

Ten people died that day from the heat. It was on the news. Ten people and Kim died that day.

I wonder if they know each other now and hold hands.

So today, at 5:48, I had to be at the rock.

And I had to be ready.

I had to believe.

In the mirror I looked like a person who could believe.

My face with my eyes and my freckles. A face I'd looked at over and over and over again for fourteen years.

Why wasn't it working?

Even with Ms. Dead Homeyer and her hair and her husband, Ed, being real, and even with Dad saying a prayer about God.

To God.

My dad.

My family.

In our house.

Even with all that, I don't think I believed.

Maybe it really was my fault.

They want to visit you. They yearn for it. You are the one stopping it. YOU.

Was it not working because of me?

I lay on my carpet and stared at the ceiling.

I could lie here all day.

I could stitch creepy dolls out of old T-shirts.

I could watch Gabby and her friends hang out in her yard in bikinis.

Or I could go find Dr. Ted Farnsworth and scream.

I stood up.

I was going to see Dr. Ted Farnsworth.

Even though I could feel the puke in my mouth.

Even though it meant going to the strip by myself.

All by myself.

Even though he was fake and creepy and a fraud.

I was going to see him because what if he wasn't a fraud?

What if he could help me?

What if this was my last chance?

I put on my red jeans that Gabby told me I should never wear.

She said it when we were getting ready to go to the mall one day. Because we went to the mall almost all the time.

"Never wear those, Emmy," she said.

"Why would you say that?" Kim asked her while I stood in the full-length mirror staring at myself in the pants I had been wearing once a week for months.

Gabby was painting her nails on our white carpet even though I asked her not to.

"I won't spill," she'd said. So she was painting her nails and Kim said, "She looks good."

Gabby looked up. Bored.

"Only certain body types can pull off colored jeans. Emmy doesn't have that body type."

Kim said, "What body type can pull it off?"

Gabby sighed. "Mine. Yours. Not Emmy's."

Kim got the look in her eyes and I said, "It's okay."

"It's not okay," she said.

"No. It's okay. I don't have to wear them," I said. Trying not to let my voice shake.

Kim said, "You're wearing them." And then to Gabby she said, "Why are you being so mean?"

"I'm not being mean. Actually I'm being nice. Friends help friends."

"You are being mean," Kim said. "You look good in the jeans," she said to me.

Gabby added a heart on her pinkie nail and said, "Do what you want, Emmy. But you don't look good. You look big."

***

I hadn't worn them since that day. Over a year ago.

But today for Kim's dead day, I was going to do whatever I wanted. I yanked them on. I couldn't button the top button, so I found a rubber band and tied the front together.

I pulled on Kim's Mickey Mouse T-shirt and braided my hair. I felt like I was preparing for something. And I guess I was.

I was preparing to go see Dr. Ted Farnsworth to change my mortal and immortal life.

• 50 •

Dr. Ted Farnsworth had a huge tour van. HUGE. A bus really.

And I said to Kim, "Look at that thing." It was black with purple nebula and stars and his huge spray-tanned face on it.

"Shh," she said.

We'd followed him out back into the blowing desert heat parking garage and now he was talking to his assistants.

The bus was towering and it made me feel uncomfortable, imagining greasy-haired Dr. Ted Farnsworth relaxing in there.

"We have to talk to him out here in the parking lot," I said. "I'm not going in that bus."

She nodded but then she said, "What could happen?"

And a lot could happen. I watched *CSI*. I watched *Law and Order*. I watched *Psych*. I even watched *Murder She Wrote* with my dad on Sundays sometimes. A lot could happen.

Finally, when his people were leaving, Kim yelled, "Dr. Ted!"

She sounded so desperate. I'd never heard Kim sound desperate.

One of his guys, the flattop one said, "He can't talk to you right now. He has to rest."

But Dr. Ted Farnsworth turned. He was standing on the steps of his bus and he turned and said, "It's okay, Bart." Then he got this huge creepy smile and said, "Come in, girls, and chat for a bit."

Kim started walking and I said, "We can't go in there."

She looked at me. "We have to."

"We can't."

"We have to," she said again. I grabbed her arm and she said, "Emmy. I'm going in there. You can come or you can stay."

And then she went into Dr. Ted Farnsworth's cosmic tour bus.

So I followed Kim inside. I couldn't let her go alone.

"Sit down, sit down, girls," he said. "Sit down."

He motioned to a leather couch against one wall of the bus.

There was a flat screen TV. A full kitchen. A massage chair. I could see a bedroom down the hall. It was awesome. And also made me sick. This guy was making a lot of money.

"You like it?" he said.

"Yeah," said Kim. "It's nice." She was sitting on the edge of the couch and I saw that she'd written some questions down.

He sat down on the massage chair and then he pointed at Kim. "So you're going to die."

HOLY CRAP. HOLY CRAP.

Kim turned white and I felt nauseous again and Dr. Ted Farnsworth said, "It's okay. It's okay, girls. It's a part of the grand scheme of things, you know what I mean?"

I tried to think what to say. What I had the courage to say. He was a jerk. And a fake. And he was full of crap and I wanted to throw a wooden duck at him. We shouldn't be in there and why did he say that? I started to stand up but Kim said, "Yeah. I am going to die. And it's okay."

"That's right," he said. "It's okay."

I looked at her. She had a determined look on her face and it scared me.

"How did you know," she said.

He leaned forward and touched her cheek with his big fat hand and said, "Darling, the beautiful touch of death is on your visage."

She started to tear up.

"What are you talking about?" I said, barely able to control myself. "What are you talking about?"

Kim said, "It's okay, Emmy. I am."

"No, you're not. Jenny Biggs lived to be fifty-four, which is really old. You're going to get really old." My voice was louder than I expected it to be, but I didn't care.

"I'm dying, Em. I am. I'm going to die," she said.

I tried to swallow but it was hard. So hard. "No you're not," I said.

She wasn't. She was not. She was fine. She looked good. She looked fine. She was *not* going to die.

"I thought things were going better," I said. Trish had told Mom that. That things were going better.

Kim nodded. "They were but . . .

Then she stopped talking like we were in a soap opera and Dr. Ted Farnsworth who was listening to me and my best friend fight about how she was going to die, Dr. Ted Farnsworth scooted back in his dumb massage chair and pushed a button, and his orange face started jiggling.

"I hope you girls don't mind if I do a little refreshing while we talk. I'm quite sore."

This was not happening.

He cleared his throat and got this serious look on his face and said to Kim, "You can feel it, can't you? You can feel death approaching."

Kim nodded. "I sort of can. Does that happen?"

I looked at her. She could feel death coming?

"Sure does," he said. "Especially to sensitive souls." He pushed another button and then his voice vibrated and he said, "So you got heart disease?"

Kim nodded—I could tell she was in shock and so was I. How did he know that?

I tried to calm myself down. Get my breathing normal. This was a mistake. She'd been going to parties with Gabby. She was voted hot bod on the student council poll week. She was maybe going to try out for the dance team.

She was not sick. This was a mistake.

He took out his iPhone and started typing things in.

"Are you excited?" he asked.

He was crazy. He was a crazy man. Excited? To die? Who was excited to die? What kind of question was that?

But then she just said, like it was normal, she just said, "I don't know."

This was the first time Kim talked about her death. I mean she'd talked about dying and her funeral and dead people and stupid stuff all the time. But not like this. Not like she was going to die tomorrow.

Then she said, "Will it hurt?"

He turned off the stupid chair and took her hand. "It might hurt. You know, initially, but then it will feel warm."

I wanted to punch him in the face. I wanted to punch him hard, and I wanted to get out of that leather and brass bus as fast as we could. But Kim, when I looked at her, she had a tear running down her cheek.

He said, "Tell me what I can do for you."

Kim shifted on the couch. She glanced at me and then she said, "I want to come back," she said. And he nodded. "As you should."

Then her voice got more confident. "This is my best

friend, Emmy. She is perfect for the medium. I think she'd be perfect for the medium."

He looked me square in the eye for the first time. "Hi, Emmy."

He waited for me to say something.

"Uh, hi, Dr. Farnsworth," I said.

"Call me Dr. Ted," he said, his big fat gold tooth glittered in the fluorescent lighting.

"Do you have what it takes to help your friend?"

I could feel Kim watching me. I could feel her staring and at that moment, I wished she had brought Gabby. Or even Joe or someone. I wished it wasn't just me.

I took a breath and then I said, "Sure."

"Sure?"

"Sure."

"Sure is not enough." He looked at Kim. "Sure is not enough."

"She can do it," Kim said. "I know she can. She's more of an iceberg, you know?"

Ugh.

He looked at me again. Cocked his head to one side and closed his eyes. "Tell me your full name."

"Emilee Anderson," I said.

"Emilee Anderson." He opened his eyes. "I think

Kimberly here is right. I think you are an iceberg. I think there's much hidden under the surface but you're afraid."

Kim nodded. "She's afraid of everything."

What? Why would she say that?

He nodded. Then he said, "But you want to see your friend again, right?"

I started to sweat. Why were we in here? Why were we here?

"Yeah, of course," I said.

He put his hand on my knee. "You can do it. You can. I feel the love between you two."

My mouth was dry and I moved my knee away from him.

"I think we should go," I said. And I stood up.

Kim didn't stand up but I said, "Come on, Kim." I said it loud and it startled her.

"What is wrong with you," she said, but I was shaking and, "We are leaving."

Dr. Ted Farnsworth laughed. "It's okay, Kimberly. Classic iceberg behavior. I have to recharge anyway. I'm going to give you some advice and a gift. First of all, you are both young. This is in your favor."

He was talking like Yoda. He was a fat, orange Yoda.

"It's much easier to cross over if you're young and you believe." He pointed to me, "You need to access your depth. You need to let go of your heart and let it breathe."

He stood up and walked to the front of the bus. "Let's go," I whispered.

"Please, Emmy. Please," she said. "Just hang on."

He came back holding a box.

He said, "This is what you really want. It's out of print."

On the front it said, *If You Believe*.

Kim opened it. It was full of old CDs. "Have your friend listen to these," he said. "It will give her the power to overcome her weaknesses and unearth her sensitivities and then," he paused for dramatic effect, "and then you two will be able to continue your relationship into the eternities."

Kim gripped the box and I said, "Come on."

And she said, "Thank you so much, doctor. So much."

And then we left.

51

The house was empty. I was about to go see Dr. Ted Farnsworth again, and I didn't even have to worry about Mom's new goal to not let me go off on my own anymore.

She was out on errands.

Dad had a late tee time.

Joe was at his friend's house.

Mom had begged me to come with her. "You shouldn't be alone today."

"I'll be fine."

She stared at me. "Come on, Ems. You can pick out whatever you want at the grocery store."

One thing is, I'm not three.

"It's okay," I told her. "I'll be okay."

So she was gone.

I wrote a note: *Gone to the library.*

Then I walked out the door into the sun and headed to the bus stop. It would take me an hour and a half to get downtown because of the Saturday bus schedule.

That gave me at least a two-hour cushion before Dr. Ted's early show at Circus Circus, Meeting Room A.

52

I had to figure out how to get Gabby to Forever 21 on her birthday.

It was coming up and I'd had no contact with Kim. None. Not even "a feeling or a warm embrace." Gabby at Forever 21 was the next date we'd agreed on.

Kim had said, "I'll meet you guys at the jewelry."

"Why the jewelry?"

Kim looked up from the calendar. "Where do you think we should meet?"

I thought about it for a second. "Gabby is always buying those maxidresses."

"Yeah," Kim said, "but they might not have maxidresses all the time. The jewelry never moves."

I hated this. I hated this.

"Okay. Won't it be too crowded?" I said.

"No," Kim said. "Remember Holly Wever?"

In *Hello from Heaven*, a girl named Holly Wever was visited by her dead dad at a Killers concert.

I still felt doubtful about all of this, which was the exact opposite of how I had to feel if I was going to be a true medium.

"And you have to get her there," Kim said. "It won't work if you don't get her there."

"What if she doesn't want to?"

"Trick her," she said.

"Trick her?"

"Yeah. All you have to do is get her there."

So, after months and months of not talking to Gabby and of being by myself and nothing, after months of all that, I tricked her.

A week before her birthday, I put a postcard in her mailbox that said, *Happy Birthday from Forever 21! Come in on your birthday and receive five free items of jewelry!!!!* I put in a lot exclamation points and used Photoshop to make it look real. At the bottom of the card I put, 50 percent off all maxidresses, just to make sure.

Then I put it in her mailbox when no one was home.

It had to work.

Five free items of jewelry? She couldn't resist.

So on the day, luckily a Saturday, I got to Meadows Mall right when it opened at ten.

I lugged the Snickers bars, the Fresca, the *Ladyhawke,* etc., etc. I brought all of it in my dad's old backpack and walked into Forever 21 when the employees were still turning on the lights.

"Welcome to Forever 21," said a girl with sexy straight hair. I was wearing a yellow Big Bird T-shirt and really bad white leggings. I was also wearing Kim's TEVAs. I did not fit in at Forever 21.

So the girl said welcome to Forever 21 and I said, "Hi," and then I pretended like I was looking at pants.

When she started folding shirts, I made my way to the jewelry.

I thought Gabby would come early. She was a major birthday girl, which meant she'd have a lot of plans. So many plans.

She'd want to hurry and get this over with.

I looked at earrings for an hour.

Then I looked at shirts.

Then I looked at earrings again.

All day long, I walked around Forever 21 with my huge backpack.

At first I was optimistic.

Then, as the day wore on, I started to feel anxious.

Maybe she figured it out. If she knew it was me she wouldn't come.

For sure.

At one point a man with no hair and tight Bermuda shorts that were quite fashionable, came over and said, "Miss? Can I help you?"

I'd been in the store for about six hours, so I didn't blame him for thinking I was a weirdo.

I said, "Yes. Do you have any dickies?"

He stared at me. "What?"

"Dickies," I said.

My mom wore dickies and it was unfortunate.

"I have to find just the right one," I said. "It's for a dickies competition."

He blinked several times and said, "You know, I can't help you." And he walked way.

✳ ✳ ✳

By eight at night I had to face the fact that she wasn't coming.

Even though I didn't think she would, I didn't think she *really* would, a part of me, in the back somewhere with the sweaters and tights, a part of me thought she would come. She'd have to come.

I almost left and then I decided to wait until they closed. What would one more hour hurt?

She didn't come.

Didn't come.

Didn't come.

Then, at eight forty, twenty minutes before closing, she walked in.

She was alone. She was wearing a romper that most people could never pull off, and she walked straight to the jewelry section.

I was sitting on the floor by the cardigans. The night manager, Megan, she'd asked me if I was okay, and I'd told her I was waiting for a friend and then she didn't seem to mind if I camped out.

I stood up as fast as I could and almost ran over to jewelry, my gigantic bag knocking some shirts off a rack.

"Gabby," I said, out of breath.

She looked up from the necklaces.

"Crap, Em. You scared me."

"Oh," I said. "Sorry."

She looked back down at the necklaces. Picked up a peacock on a chain.

"Gabby," I said.

"What?"

"It's your birthday."

"I know." She put the peacock on and walked over to the mirror. I followed her too close behind.

"Can I . . ."

I stopped

She looked at me in the mirror. "Did you give me the postcard?"

I said, "Uh."

She turned around. "What are you doing? What is going on?"

And then she said, flicking my bag, "What is this? What is in the backpack? You are turning so freaky."

I stood there.

A bead of sweat formed on her perfect forehead and I said, "Okay."

And she said, "Okay? Okay? What does that mean? Okay?" Her voice got loud. "I wasn't going to come. I knew you made that stupid card. I saw you put it in my mailbox *(crap)* and I thought this is sad. This is really really sad. Everyone thinks you're crazy, Em. Everyone. I thought, I should help poor Emmy. I should help you. But then I thought, screw that. You didn't even like the deer I made you and you act like you're the only one who misses her. You're selfish."

I'm selfish.

I'm selfish.

I'm selfish.

A lady named Betsy who I helped fold shirts for an hour, she came over and said, "Is everything okay?"

Gabby said, "Uh. No. Get away from us."

Betsy looked at me with concern and I nodded. "It's okay."

Then I said, "I'm selfish."

No I didn't. Instead I just stood there while Betsy walked away.

Gabby said, "I wasn't going to come. I had plans. But then all day I couldn't stop thinking about how pathetic you are. How sad your life is."

Then she said it. She said this: "Kim wouldn't want you to be like this."

I watched her mouth move and I felt like I was falling. I felt like I was falling in a bucket of pudding, but it was pistachio pudding which I hate, and Gabby was on the rim of the bucket and she was saying, *how sad your life is, how sad your life is, how said your life is* and I said, "KIM."

"Kim? Where are you?"

"Emmy, did you hear me? She wouldn't want you to be like this."

When she was done talking and they had come on the intercom and said they were closing, when all that happened, I said, "Gabby?"

And she said, "What?"

I tried to say something. I tried to say, Will you help me talk to Kim? Will you help me? Or maybe, I'm sorry. Maybe I tried to say I'm sorry.

But instead I just stood there.

Gabby left Forever 21.

I knocked over a tray of rings.

I didn't see Kim that day either.

• 53 •

I sometimes feel like I'm a dot.

A dot in the middle of millions and millions of other dots. Dots holding babies. Dots wearing bikinis. Dots on bikes. Dots in sports cars. Dots eating Doritos. Dots calling me fat. Dots on horses. Dots on buses.

Dots watching me. Me watching dots.

Dots.

I sat there. Once again on a city bus, a tiny tiny dot.

Dot.

A dot watching strip malls and golf courses and Hummers and palm trees and GET CASH NOW places pass by. Like it was a normal day.

Today is a normal day and I am a dot.

Kim was a dot, too, I guess, but it never felt that way. She felt like much more than a dot.

My phone buzzed.

I looked at it. Skeeter.

I stared at his name. I could answer it. I could ask him to come.

He would come.

I should tell him to come.

But then I knew he felt bad for me and I was pathetic.

I turned it off.

I could do this.

• 54 •

On the ride back from Dr. Ted Farnsworth Perry said, "How was it?"

I looked out the window and Kim said, "Great. It was great."

"What was it about again?" Perry asked. "Some kind of skin care thing?"

I looked at Kim and she said, "It was essential oils."

Perry nodded. He smiled at Kim. He smiled how everyone smiled at her, like he loved her and wished she loved him back. He didn't know she was dying.

What if he did? Would he still love her?

When they dropped me off I said to Kim, "Are you coming in?"

"No," she said. "I think I'll go home."

I wanted her to come in. I wanted her to come in and never leave. To just stay with us. Safe.

"I'm tired," she said.

"Okay," I said.

Then I watched them drive away.

That night I messaged her.

"Are you okay?"

"You forgot to take the CDs," she said.

"Oh, yeah."

I didn't want the CDs and I knew she knew it.

"Do you really not want to do this?"

I stared at the computer.

"I don't think we need to," I wrote.

"Em," she said. "We do."

I sat there.

Then she said, "Good news though."

"What?"

"I found a link."

"What?"

She sent it to me. THE GREAT JOURNEY THROUGH DEATH.

"What is this?"

"Click on it," she said.

The website was purple, with yellow type and horrible. It said when you die these things happen:

1.   Your body turns off. The organs completing their missions, one by one.
2.   Your spirit departs from the body during the rigor mortis stage.
3.   Your spirit could go to a white light if the soul has been properly prepared.
4.   Your spirit could possibly enter another body to teach lessons of love and awareness.
5.   Your spirit could enter the realm of cosmos, becoming a part of heaven and earth.
6.   Or your soul could perish.

Then it said, BUT DON'T DESPAIR! CAN YOUR TECHNOLOGY PURIFY AND CLEANSE YOUR EXISTENCE, PREPARING YOU FOR THE GREAT UNKNOWN? and there was tiny computer flashing in the corner and it said, click here to see how!

"Wow," I typed.

"I know," she said.

"Did you click on it?"

"Not yet," she said. "I thought we could click on it together."

I smiled. "Okay. Click on it in three seconds."

I moved the mouse over the opening and closing door. I counted to three and then I clicked.

The screen turned bright blue and started moving up, flying up. There were cartoon angels with harps and doves and people singing and priests holding Bibles and bouquets of flowers and then more angels.

"Wow," I typed again.

"I know," she said. "Amazing."

The screen kept scrolling up and up with more and more images of angels and birds.

Kim said, "I guess my spirit is prepared now for the great unknown."

"Yeah," I said. "I guess mine, too."

"Do you see the angels kissing?" she said.

"Yep. And the flamingo wearing a tiara?"

For an hour, Kim and I watched the sky flying up on our laptops.

"I think it's going to be okay," I said.

"Okay," she said.

· 55 ·

Right when we got to the strip, the bus driver made an announcement.

The bus is having problems. We all have to get off early.

My stomach flipped. We were nowhere near Circus Circus.

In fact, we were in front of the Bellagio, blocks and blocks away.

You can take another bus, he said on the intercom and he was going to give us free transfers.

This stressed me out.

I didn't know what bus.

Everyone was standing up and things were loud and it

meant I'd have to spend way more time on the strip than I'd planned.

On my way to the door a lady handed me an orange.

I looked at her.

"Have a happy day," she said.

"Okay," I said. I was going to have a happy day.

So I got off the bus and stood on the sidewalk, holding an orange.

I felt strange, like something was going to happen.

And then it did.

As the exhaust and heat cleared, across the street I saw her again.

Across the street I saw Ms. Dead Homeyer.

Wearing a sombrero.

A HOT BABES DIRECT TO YOU! truck drove by and when it was gone, so was she.

This was not a happy day.

• 56 •

After our visit with Dr. Ted Farnsworth, everything seemed different.

It was the same, but different.

She could feel death coming.

It was on her visage.

He knew.

She knew.

Why didn't I know?

• 57 •

I stood on the sidewalk with thousands of people pushing past me.

Thousands.

It was spring break time but I'd never ever seen the strip like this.

Not at eleven in the morning.

Not in this heat.

A group of guys in suits. A silver-painted cowboy. Forty-five band kids. Ladies in Bermuda shorts with pink sunglasses. A man yelling that the world was going to end. Babies crying. A woman walking dogs.

In the middle of all this I stood.

Ms. Dead Homeyer had been there. Right in front of Paris Las Vegas. In a sombrero.

And now she was gone.

Did this mean I was doing the right thing? Was Ms. Dead Homeyer going to come back? Sing more Fun in my ear?

I waited to see if she would reappear. Come tell me what to do.

But she didn't.

Instead I was scorching my neck and I needed to move. I turned toward Circus Circus and almost ran straight into a tall man wearing tall pants, who had a mole the size of Texas on his face.

I gasped.

He swore at me. "Get out of the way."

But I was frozen.

"You going to get out of the way?" he said.

It was Kim's uncle Sid.

Kim's dead uncle Sid that I said I'd never want to see naked.

Ever.

He went around me and disappeared into the crowd.

At least he wasn't naked.

• 58 •

Sometimes it feels like my whole life before she died was a dream.

Sometimes it feels like I'm floating.

Floating down a river and an alligator says to me, did you know hippos are more dangerous than me?

And I say, what about sharks?

And he says, sharks will bite off your legs and I say, yes. Yes. They will.

Nothing made sense now.

I walked down the street.

And walked and walked.

Was that really Uncle Sid? Or was I hallucinating?

I had to focus. Get to the seminar. He would explain. Dr. Ted Farnsworth would explain. There was nothing in the book about this, nothing even close.

All these people.

People everywhere.

I walked slowly, trying not to touch anyone, which was impossible.

A lady handed me a flyer with a lady on it that I stuffed in my pocket. I knew what it was and I didn't want to even look at it, but I also didn't want to throw it on the ground with the thousands and thousands of other pieces of paper.

A kid was crying about a sucker.

And then I saw a woman who looked like my mom's Jenny Craig counselor, the one who died of cancer.

Was it her?

I couldn't be sure. I'd only seen her a few times.

Like twice.

But it looked like her. It looked exactly like her. She was laughing with other ladies at a café table.

I kept walking.

Things were slowing down and then speeding up. People coming near me. Their faces animated and huge. Then shrinking. Like I was in a fun house.

Did I recognize them? Had I seen them before?

But then the strip always felt like this to me. Surreal and odd.

Now it was just more complicated.

A man with a cane and suspenders who looked like our old neighbor Harry who'd had a heart attack, and Mom and Dad had to help clean out his house.

But it wasn't him. It didn't even look like him. It wasn't him.

Or maybe it was.

What if everyone *was* dead? What if that's why I didn't like it down here? Maybe all along, the strip was for walking dead people.

Was I dead? Did I die on that bus? Did I die last night? At Ms. Dead Homeyer's funeral?

Was I going to be stuck on the strip forever?

I stopped for a second to catch my breath. I tried to not think about the swirling around me but it was impossible.

Everyone laughing, talking as loud as they could, across the street, the Cheesecake Factory with a line of dead people waiting to get in and stuff their faces.

Then there was a car.

A low rider Cadillac with one side higher than the other.

Rap music blaring and a man, a huge man, driving. One arm on the steering wheel, the other out the window.

Fatbutt.

I was going crazy. I was going completely crazy.

Just then a man dressed as the Statue of Liberty knocked into me and I dropped my orange.

I had almost forgotten I had it until it fell and when I saw it hit the ground, a panic came over me.

I needed that orange.

I needed it.

The orange was real. It was hard and real and if I peeled it, I could eat it.

And if I ate it, and the juice would go down my throat and into my stomach. If that happened, I could not be dead. Right?

I chased after it, weaving through people.

It kept rolling and rolling and rolling, like it had a life of its own.

Flip-flops, boots, sandals, tennis shoes, and the orange rolled on.

And on.

And on.

Until finally, after more than half a block, it rested at the toe of a pair of green Pumas.

I looked up.

It was the zitty boy. From Ms. Dead Homeyer's funeral.

A reunion.

I took a breath.

"Hey," he said.

"Hey," I said.

I grabbed the orange and stood.

We both stared at each other. I thought I should be scared of him. That this meant something but for some reason I felt a calm come over me. A calm that I needed.

"You gonna eat that?" he said.

I looked at the orange in my hand that I was gripping a lot harder than I realized. Squeezing.

"I don't know."

"I think you should."

"You do?"

"I do."

"Okay," I said.

And then me and the boy from Pal's mortuary became friends.

• 60 •

We were in front of Treasure Island, me and the kid from Pal's.

He sat down right there on the pathway up to a pirate ship under a sign with sexy girls that said:

COME SEE THE SIRENS OF TREASURE ISLAND!!
Be enchanted by the beautiful temptresses as they lure
a band of renegade pirates with their mesmerizing
melodies of seduction and danger!!!

Free shows nightly!

Parental Guidance suggested—strollers not permitted.

"You're sitting here? On the sidewalk?"

"There's nowhere else to sit," he said.

And it was true. There were no benches on the strip. They didn't want you to rest or relax or talk. They wanted you to go inside and lose all your money and get drunk. Or stand and watch temptresses lure men into seduction and danger.

I sat next to him.

"I've been waiting for you," he said.

It was a weird thing to say.

"You have?" I said, trying to sound fine about that.

"Yep."

"Why? How did you know I'd be here?"

He shrugged. "I don't know."

"You don't know?"

"I just knew."

I wiped the sweat from my upper lip.

"You didn't remember me," he said.

"You mean from the funeral?" I said.

He shook his head. "No. Not from the funeral."

"From when?"

"From before," he said.

I was confused. The first time I'd seen him was outside Pal's.

"I don't know you," I said.

245

He started untying his shoes and then tying them back up. Untying again.

I watched him. He was doing it slowly, with precision.

Ms. Dead Homeyer had played with her shoelaces, too. What did it mean?

Then he said, "I know you."

I came out of my trance. "What?"

"You're Joe Anderson's sister."

My heart pounded.

"You know Joe?" I said.

He nodded. "And I know you."

"How?"

He looked at me.

"Who do you think I am?"

I stared at his face. His zits. He *did* look familiar. Sort of. Barely.

I had no idea.

"It's okay," he said.

"It's okay?"

"Yeah. It's okay."

"Then who are you?"

He sighed. "I'm kind of famous."

Now I was really confused.

He pulled out of his pocket a crumpled brochure of New York-New York casino.

It had been opened and reopened so many times the edges were white and looked like they were about to tear.

What?

"Look," he said. He unfolded it. There was a schematic of the roller coaster. He'd circled areas and there were figures and diagrams and notes all over the place.

I stared at it. And then I realized.

"No," I said.

He laughed.

"No."

"Yes."

"You're Baylor?"

I could see his face now, his smiling face in the obituary.

Baylor Frederick Hicks, the boy my brother had bet on. RIP.

• 61 •

One time a boy called me.
   He said, "Hey."
   I said, "Hey."

And then he said nothing.

For a long, long time.

At first it was a little romantic, maybe.

But then it was weird.

And then I knew it was a prank call or something worse. A murderer.

Right when I was about to hang up, he said, "Emmy."

He sounded nervous.

"Hi," I said.

"Are you okay?"

Was I okay?

"Yeah," I said.

"Is this a good time to talk?"

Who was this? Who could it be?

"Yeah. Sure."

Then he said, "My mom heard from your mom that Kim is pretty sick."

"What?"

He said it again, "Your mom told my mom about Kim."

"Who is this?" I said.

"Oh," he said. "Sorry. This is Skeeter."

Ugh. Skeeter.

He kept talking. "I just wanted to tell you that I know and that I'm sorry and I don't know. I know we don't really hang out but I thought I'd just call and I, it's probably stupid . . ."

His voice trailed off.

Skeeter had called me one other time in my life and that was when Kim accidentally took his hoodie when we were in elementary school and we'd played night games at the park and he was scared his mom was going to kill him.

"Okay," I said.

"Okay," he said.

And that was it.

• 62 •

He looked different. Very different.

His hair was bigger, his face was bigger, everything felt bigger.

In the obituary picture he looked like a little boy. A scared little boy and this kid did not seem scared at all, not one bit. But it was him. I could see it now. It was the same person.

Baylor Frederick Hicks.

I was confused.

What am I doing, Kim? Where am I? What is happening?

But of course, she didn't answer back. Didn't send a thought or a feeling. Nothing.

He started fiddling with his watch. A purple Swatch.

"I can't get this dumb thing to work," he said.

I said . . .

He said . . .

I said . . .

He said, "Do you know how to work this?"

He held the watch to my face. "Uh. No."

"Ugh," he said.

Then I said, "You're dead?"

"Yep."

He kept fiddling, put the watch back on. I sat there. So many questions were crowding in my head, I didn't know where to start so I said, "Does it hurt?"

The same question Kim had asked Dr. Ted Farnsworth.

He looked at me. "Does what hurt? The watch?"

"No. Being dead."

"Oh," he said. "Oh. Nope. Not now."

He took the Swatch off again and studied it.

Something started to build in my stomach. Something small that grew into a full-blown ache.

"Am I dead?" I asked.

He looked at me. "What?"

"Am I dead? Is everyone here dead?"

He laughed. "No."

"No?"

"No. But there are lots of dead people."

"Really?"

"Yeah. There are lots of dead people everywhere."

I felt numb. "There are?"

"Of course," he said.

"Why?"

"Why what?"

"Why are there dead people everywhere?"

He thought about it for a minute. Then he said, "I think they're all trying to figure something out. Doing things. Watching people. Finishing stuff."

I swallowed. Kim could really be here. She could be on a gondola in the Venetian or looking at sharks at Mandalay Bay.

He put the watch back on and there are dead people everywhere. Trying to figure something out. Did Kim need to figure something out?

"Do they stay here forever?" I asked.

"No. They leave."

"When?"

He shrugged. "I don't know yet. I'm still here."

"Why?"

He was quiet for a minute. "I don't know."

"Oh."

My head started to pound and I felt a little dizzy.

"Are you okay?"

I swallowed. "Uh. I don't think so."

He nodded. "You don't have to be okay."

I looked at him. "What?"

"You don't have to be okay," he said again. "Most people aren't."

And I said, "Thank you."

63

Once when I was bored, I googled Axl Rose and Slash and I don't even care and I don't listen to Guns N' Roses, but one day Skeeter said to me, "Axl Rose has a lot of hate."

We were sitting at the same table we always sat at and not talking when he just blurted it out, like it was a crucial piece of information. He said, "Axl Rose has a lot of hate."

I said, "Who is Axl Rose?"

And he told me that Axl Rose was the lead singer of Guns N' Roses and the band was supposed to be inducted into the Rock and Roll Hall of Fame but Axl won't come because Slash will be there.

"Who's Slash?"

"The guitarist. The original guitarist."

"Who's Axl?"

"The singer."

"And why won't he come?"

"Axl won't come because Slash would be there."

"Why?"

"They hate each other."

"They hate each other? But they were in the same band."

"Yep. Best friends for a bit. But not anymore."

"Why?"

"A bunch of reasons. Axl actually used to live with Slash and then he slept on Slash's grandma's couch and when the grandma wanted to sit on her couch, you know, she couldn't."

I stared at Skeeter. "Why are you telling me this?"

He said, "Here," and he put his headphones in my ear and I listened to "Welcome to the Jungle."

When the song was over I took off the headphones and said, "Never do that again."

"You loved it."

"No. I didn't love that song."

"You did."

But I didn't.

Maybe I did.

I googled Guns N' Roses and fight and Slash and Axl Rose and now I know everything.

This is the kind of really important thing I would like to discuss with Kim.

64

Five pirates walked past us.

I wondered how you got to be a sexy pirate at Pirate Island. I wondered if they were dead sexy pirates. I also wondered if Gabby should try out.

I looked at Baylor. I had two big questions for him. The first one was about me. The second one was about Kim.

"So you said you knew me?"

"Yep. We met. Lots of times."

I stared at him. We hadn't. We didn't. I would remember.

"When?" I asked.

"At your brother's games."

"Joe's games?"

He nodded.

I racked my brain. No one went to those stupid sopho-more games except for parents and bored cheerleaders and sad people who wanted extra credit or liked someone on the team. If this kid, if Baylor Frederick Hicks had been there, I would have remembered. I was sure of it.

He laughed at me. "You look confused."

"I am confused," I said. Sweat was dripping down my face now and I was getting sunburned. Baylor on the other hand, didn't seem affected. Maybe dead people didn't get heat stroke.

"I was sort of hidden," he said.

Hidden? What was he talking about?

"I'll show you," he said.

"You'll show me?"

"Yeah," he said. "I'll show you."

He stood up. Walked to the middle of the sidewalk, closed his eyes and then, this really happened, then he started doing the robot. Right there. In front of Pirate Island. On the strip.

He was good.

Really good.

Like better than anyone I'd seen.

At one point he made a motion showing his heart beating,

his chest going in and out, his hand mimicking his chest. I'd seen that move before.

I'd seen it at the games.

And then I realized.

"Wait a second. Are you . . ."

He kept going. Doing a signature moonwalk and then I knew for sure.

I couldn't believe it but I knew it.

Baylor Frederick Hicks was the panther mascot for Palo Verde High.

65

You can love someone you don't know.

I know this is true because once I saw a boy at Yellowstone and we both looked at each other across the geyser and he smiled and I smiled and then his mom said, "For the last time, Jared, get in the car!" and he was gone.

For three years I thought about Jared.

And before Jared from Yellowstone I loved a real boy. It was sixth grade and his name was Isaac and he always wore shorts, even on the fifth-grade field trip up the mountains.

He played soccer and one time he accidentally smooshed my sculpture in art.

So then I accidentally smooshed his.

He threw some clay at me and I started to laugh. I'm sorry but I did.

So then I threw it at him.

Everyone was watching.

Then we got in trouble.

Kim said, "You like him."

And I said, "No I don't. He's so gross."

The next day I told him he was a jerk and he said I was a butt, and secretly, deep down, I knew, I knew knew knew that someday we would get married. Or at least kiss.

But then, and I didn't really care, but one day, during lunch recess, Kim got a note from Candace Perkins who got the note from Janni Kimball who got the note from Eric Freeman who was Isaac's best friend.

It said:

> Kim. Will you go out with me?
> YES NO MAYBE
> From Isaac.

* * *

Me and Kim and Candace Perkins and two other girls read it on the blacktop by the bars, and Candace said, "Oh my gosh," and Kim was bright red and she looked at me and I didn't look at her.

Later she said, "I might say yes."

My face burned. "You like him?" I asked.

"I don't know," she said. "Maybe."

We were walking home and I was kicking a rock hard down the sidewalk.

"Are you mad?" she asked.

I tried to keep my voice steady. "No."

"Are you sure?"

"Yeah. I don't care. I think he's dumb."

She nodded. "You think he's gross."

"Yeah," I said.

So Kim went out with Isaac for one month and that meant they never talked and he bought her a ring at Santa's Secret Shop and she got him a Gak ball and one time, on a Saturday night, we had to walk to the park, and she went to the middle of the field while I waited, and he went to the middle of the field while his friend waited, and then they had their first kiss.

When I got home, I cried the whole night.

I sat in my closet.

They broke up the next week.

I wonder why she didn't know. How did she not know? We knew everything about each other. Why would she do that to me? But then, maybe she didn't know.

Sometimes I buy bags of Cinnamon Bears.
  Or Peach Rings.
  Starbursts.
  Skittles.

Gummy Worms.

Sour Patch Kids.

Runts.

Red Vines.

Bags and bags and bags.

Sometimes I imagine my spine is lined with gummy fruit, and when they cut me open to see how I died, they'll sit and eat for days.

"You are so good!"

"I'm not that good," Baylor said, sitting back down next to me. He said that but you could tell he knew he was good.

"You did the worm on the floor," I said. "With that huge mascot head on."

He nodded. "Yep. That wasn't even hard."

"It wasn't?"

"Nope."

"But Joe never told me you were . . ." I stopped. Then I tried again. "No one ever . . . no one said you were the mascot. Like in the news articles and things."

I didn't say obituary. News articles.

"Yeah," he said. "I'm sure it wasn't mentioned."

"But wouldn't that have helped?" I asked.

I should have stopped talking. I just thought, you know, the mascot was cool. He was my favorite part of Joe's stupid games. Even Dad made a comment about the panther and that was saying something.

"Helped what?" he said.

"I uh, I," I tried to answer the question. I wanted to say that maybe things wouldn't have gone so wrong if people knew he was the mascot. Maybe someone would have talked him out of riding the roller coaster. I mean even butthead Tony would have to respect someone who could not only do the robot but pop and lock like a pro all while wearing a hairy black cat costume.

"I know what you're trying to say," he said as a huge stretch white limo passed. "No one knew because the real mascot paid me twenty bucks to do the sophomore and girls' games for him, but I couldn't tell anyone it was me. He did all the varsity stuff and practiced with the cheerleaders."

I stared at him. "Really?"

He nodded. "It was my little secret."

"But didn't you want people to know?"

He shrugged. "I like to dance but not in front of people—especially not at school. I sort of hate people to tell you the truth."

I shifted on the sidewalk.

He hated people.

I thought about Joe calling him a loser. I thought about fat-face Tony. I thought maybe I hated people, too.

Did I hate people?

"Why do you hate people?" I asked.

He shrugged. "I'm not like everyone else. And people don't really like me."

He got quiet.

We both got quiet.

Finally I said, "I like you," which was so stupid because I didn't even know him but I always, always loved the panther.

He smiled. "Thanks. I like you, too," he said. He hesitated and then he said, "I watched for you every game."

My heart jumped. Was he serious?

The mascot *had* paid a lot of attention to us. Mom even commented on how strange it was that he kept coming over and shaking our hands. Now I knew it was because of me.

Or maybe Kim. Kim came to the games sometimes, too.

"What about the girl with the long black hair?" I said.

"Who?"

"Kim Porter?"

He shrugged. "I don't know who you're talking about."

I sat there for a second. He had looked for me. He was really talking about me. I felt hot and nervous and weird and I wished I could do the robot.

Then I got a hold of myself. "She's dead," I said.

"What?"

"She's dead."

"Oh," he said.

"Are you sure you don't know her?"

I showed him a picture of Kim on my phone and he shook his head. "Sorry. I don't."

A large man walked up and stood right between us, leaning over the rope fence looking at the pirate ship.

He was eating a gigantic taco.

I was almost grateful for the break so I could get everything together in my head. Never in all my life had a boy watched out for me. And he didn't know Kim. Even dead Kim.

I took a breath and leaned forward so I could see him.

Baylor waved.

I waved back.

The man looked down at me and then looked at ghost Baylor, who he obviously couldn't see, and then back at me. I didn't think the man was dead.

He felt alive.

And I was alive.

But Baylor was dead.

• 67 •

Less than a week before she died, Kim was supposed to come over and watch *Hairspray.*

We watched it once a month and ate popcorn and made Coke floats.

It was our tradition.

I was getting everything ready when she called and said she wasn't feeling so great.

"What's wrong?"

"It's nothing big," she said. "Just, you know, sort of nauseous."

I drew a circle on a piece of paper. Over and over again.

"So you can't come?"

She was quiet. Then she said, "I could but I'd probably be puking the whole time."

I closed my eyes. I hated her heart.

"Okay," I said. "Do you want me to come over? Bring you something?"

"No," she said. "I just want to sleep."

"Okay," I said, and that was it. I thought that was it.

But then, Dad talked me into going to Smiths with him to buy some Cheese Whiz for nachos. I wasn't going to go because I was in my pajamas already and about to watch the movie but he promised me he'd buy me a bag of Starburst Jelly Beans, which I love.

"And some Twizzlers," he said.

"Really, Dad? Twizzlers? You're going for the big guns."

He laughed and so I went with him.

And then this happened: I was there, in the candy aisle, when I heard them. They were laughing and talking about a party and I heard her.

I heard Kim's voice.

I froze. A boy was saying something. Then she said, "Shut up!" And then there was more laughing.

I looked down the aisle and they were at the end by the yogurt and sour cream.

I died. I died right then. It was Kim and Gabby and some guys from school.

A big group.

One of them was trying to pick Kim up and she was screaming, and Gabby was holding some other guy's hand and I pulled my hoodie up over my head and put my head between the Gummy Worms and Peach Rings, adrenaline rushing.

What if they came to get candy? What if they walked right up to me? What was I going to do?

But then they kept going, the laughing dying as they moved away.

And I kept standing there. Cinnamon Bears, chocolate-covered almonds, Bit-O-Honeys. I stood there and tried not to cry. Tried not to cry.

When Dad found me, I was still in the candy.

"Are you okay?"

I nodded.

"Emmy. What's wrong?"

I shook my head.

"Tell me."

I shook my head harder, tears streaming down my face.

"Do you want your jelly beans?"

"No," I whispered.

"You don't?"

"No."

He put a bag in the cart anyway. And three bags of Twizzlers.

Then we went home and I sat in my closet and ate all of it at once.

• 68 •

The large man standing between Baylor and me ate his taco and then dropped his wrapper on the ground and walked away.

When he was gone, Baylor said, "You ever tried a burrito over there?"

I looked across the street. Smashed in between stores and casinos and clubs was a tiny pink stucco building with bars on the windows, a flamingo on the sign that said BETOS TACO SHOP, and a couple of tables on the sidewalk.

I'd never noticed it before but then I never came down here.

"So?" he said. "You ever tried one?"

"No," I said. "And I don't think I want to."

"You do," he said. "They're the best."

"They are?"

"Oh yeah. You'll see."

He stood up.

I'll see? I didn't want a burrito. Actually I did want a burrito. I was hungry. I looked at my watch. One thirty. I had less than an hour before Dr. Ted Farnsworth was going to speak.

"Wait," I said. "Wait!"

But it was too late.

He was already dodging taxis and limos and Girls Gone Wild trucks, running across the street.

He walked into the taco shop. Just walked in like he was alive and fine and could buy a burrito.

He walked in and then a few minutes later he walked out and with him was a man.

Crowds of people moved in front of them, but there was definitely Baylor and a man.

A willowy guy with a baseball hat and a beard and a big brown bag. He looked confused.

And nervous.

He walked toward the light at the intersection. Baylor walked with him, practically arm in arm. The man kept glancing over at me and then quickly looking away.

The two of them crossed the street. The man hesitated and then started walking toward Pirate Island. I stood up. I don't know why.

When he got to me he almost stopped. Almost. But then he kept going.

Baylor said, "We'll be right back."

"Okay," I said.

A lady with a fanny pack looked at me.

I didn't look at her. Instead, I kept focused on dead Baylor and his new friend.

They walked to the end of the block and then the man and Baylor turned around. The man stood there for a minute. I acted like I wasn't watching.

Like I wasn't entranced by what was happening.

Baylor smiled even though the man clearly was in distress.

The man started back toward me and I inspected my nails. Finally he approached.

"Hello," the man said, his voice gruff.

I said, "Hello."

He said, "This may seem strange but . . ."

He stopped.

I waited.

He chewed on his lip. Then he said, "I bought you something."

Baylor was beaming.

"Oh," I said.

"Yeah," he said. He reached into the bag and pulled out a steaming package wrapped in yellow paper.

"It's the Texano," the man said. "I've never even tried it but I had this distinct impression that you, the pretty girl sitting across the street, needed a Texano burrito."

Pretty girl? Me? Baylor was blushing and I was probably blushing.

"Did you need a Texano burrito?" the man asked.

It seemed like he really wanted to know.

"I mean," he said, "were you waiting for a Texano burrito?"

I wasn't sure what to say but then Baylor mouthed Y E S so I said, "Yes."

"Yes?" the man said.

"Yes," I said.

"Yes?"

"Uh, I guess. I don't know."

He studied my face and I tried to just be calm. Holding a hot burrito.

Then he said, "Okay."

And I said, "Okay."

And he turned and walked back down the street, across the intersection, and into a crowd of people.

I looked at Baylor. "Could he see you?" I asked.

"Nope."

"So he wasn't dead?"

"Nope."

"How did you do that?"

He shrugged. "I just gave him the idea and helped him follow through."

I laughed. "Really?"

"Really."

"Is it hard?"

He shrugged and then motioned to the burrito. "Eat," he said.

"You didn't have to do that."

Baylor sat down. I sat back down next to him. "You really didn't," I said.

"Take a bite."

"You freaked him out."

"Take a bite," he said again.

I unwrapped the burrito. I was more than hungry. I was starving. Which reminded me that I was in a hurry.

"What time is it?"

He held up his arm to show me his broken watch.

"I sort of have to be somewhere soon."

"Take a bite take a bite take a bite."

I looked at it. "It's called the Texano?"

279

"It's the best burrito they make, sort of secret though."

No one had ever bought me food before. And never a secret special burrito.

I held it to my nose like I was on TV.

"Smells good, eh?"

"We'll see," I said, I guess sort of flirting which is gross. Is it gross? I had never flirted before and never with a dead guy, but then I thought maybe that was good practice.

I wondered if dead people could kiss. Then I knew I was really gross. But can they?

"Eat it before it gets cold," he said.

So I took a bite.

Baylor was watching my face and I didn't want to let him down and I wasn't going to let him down because it *was* the best burrito I had ever had, and when I was done chewing he said, "See?"

And I said, "You're so right," and he laughed.

So I ate a burrito with Dead Baylor Frederick Hicks. We talked about the taco shop and how no one would ever eat there with him.

"They wouldn't?"

"No," he said. "Not my parents. Not my friends. No one. There's one up in Summerlin and I'd try to get people to go there."

"Where in Summerlin?"

"By the Las Vegas Athletic Club," he said.

I nodded. I knew exactly where he was talking about. Kim would have loved this.

He kept going. "No one believed me about how good it was because the restaurants look beat down."

"It does look beat down," I said.

I took another bite. Then with my mouth half full, I said, "I would have eaten there with you."

He smiled. "I agree. I think you would have."

We talked about doing the robot and how he learned most of his moves on YouTube.

We talked about the school science fair and how he got the prize taken away because they said he cheated.

"What?"

"Yeah," he said. "They said it was too advanced. There's no way I could have come up with it myself."

I stared at him. He was smart. And he was funny. And he could dance. But he was also dead.

"What did you do?"

He shrugged. "I argued with them and called one judge a buttwipe."

"What? You did?"

"Yep."

"What did your parents do?"

"Nothing."

"Nothing?"

"They work a lot."

"Oh," I said.

"Yeah," he said.

I took another bite and then I said, "I actually really have to go."

"Where?"

So I told him about Dr. Ted Farnsworth. I told him about the seminar. About Kim. About how today was an important day.

He listened and then when I was done, I thought he'd say it was hopeless. Or tell me Dr. Ted Farnsworth was a joke. Or that it was a waste of my time and I was stupid. I thought he'd say something like that, but instead he said, "I'll walk you there. You need to hurry," and he stood up.

• 69 •

Nothing would ever be the same.

Ever.

I knew it.

But she didn't.

I knew it so bad that I sat in the bathroom Monday after I'd seen them at the store.

I sat in the first stall of a girls' bathroom, and I sat there and sat there and sat there.

I saw Kim in the hallway, she and Gabby were talking and they were waiting for me and I couldn't do it.

I couldn't do it.

So I turned and went the other way.

I skipped all three classes we had together.

Kim texted me. And called me and texted me.

And called.

Even Gabby texted around lunch. `R U OK? Kim is freaking out.`

I sat there in the bathroom stall and memorized the wall.

Sally Henley is a b.

Call me!

U R A SUCKAZ.

I wondered who wrote *U R A SUCKAZ*. And Was I a suckaz? What made someone a suckaz?

I sat there all day and I waited until the janitor knocked on the door in the afternoon to come in to clean it. I waited that long to leave and then when he came in, I came out and he said, "Oh. I'm sorry. I didn't know anyone was in here" and I said, "No one was in here."

I avoided Kim.

Then the next day she collapsed.

• 70 •

Baylor walked fast, so fast I had to almost run to catch up.

It was tricky because we were both dodging people, though I wondered if he could walk through them if he wanted.

I also wondered why he was so anxious for me to get there on time. And then I wondered if this meant Dr. Ted Farnsworth had been the real thing the whole time.

Baylor even said, "You should have told me sooner," and I said, "I tried to."

And he said, "Sorry. Sometimes I'm not so good at letting people talk."

We wove in and out and in and out until, before I could

even think, we were standing under the gigantic Circus Circus sign.

"We're here," he said.

I felt sick. So sick I thought I needed to sit down.

"You should go," he said.

"You're not coming?"

He shook his head. "No. I don't think so."

I swallowed. "Okay."

Then he said, "I want to tell you something."

I looked at him, trying to stop myself from shaking.

He took a long time to get his words together.

Finally he cleared his throat and said, "I wanted to tell you that I didn't die because of the loop part of the track on the roller coaster."

I stared at him. He stared at me. "Do you understand?"

"No," I said. "What are you talking about?"

"This is important. I didn't die because my physics was off. I died because I had an asthma attack and couldn't get the restraint back on in time."

It took me awhile to respond because I didn't know what to say. This felt like a big deal. A very big deal.

He said, "Are you okay?"

I nodded. "Are you okay?"

And he said, "I am now."

"You are now?"

And he said, "Do you believe me?"

And I said, "Why wouldn't I believe you?"

He smiled. He smiled huge and he said, "Thank you."

And I said, "For what?"

And he said, "Just everything. I wish we'd known each other when I was alive."

I felt myself get hot. "I wish that, too."

He reached toward my cheek and I stiffened, which was stupid, but was he going to touch me?

He put his hand down. "Thank you," and then he said something. He said, "You know your friend? The one from the funeral place?"

"Skeeter?"

He shrugged. "Whatever his name is."

"Yeah."

"I like him."

"You like him?"

"Yeah," he said. "I do."

I had no idea what this had to do with anything.

"I have to go," he said.

"Where are you going?"

And he said, "I will never ever ever forget you, okay? I will never forget you. I've always known you were special. And you just changed my life."

"I what?"

But then it was too late.

He was gone.

• 71 •

There are a lot of things I don't understand.

Like the time I found my mom sobbing in the car in the garage. Or the time my brother, Joe, left the house for three days and no one said anything about it. Or the time Dad decided not to run the 10K he'd been training for eight months to do.

I don't understand why armpit hair grows so fast or why boys stand in groups and throw things at people.

I don't understand how you can be so close to someone, so close that they know you wet the bed until you were ten. And then feel so, so, so far away.

* * *

One time, my heart was floating on a raft in the middle of the ocean. The waves moving it up and down and up and down. The sun beating and I said, *Dear heart. I hate you. I hope you die.*

I hope you die.

• 72 •

I stood in front of the casino too long.

Baylor was gone. People were going in and out. The whole world spinning. I can do this. I can do this. I can do this.

Then I went inside Circus Circus to go find Dr. Ted Farnsworth.

• 73 •

If your best friend is long and skinny and boys start to notice her but not you because you blend into the dirt, you could get sad.

I'd been sad at her before.

Like one time I was sad because I don't even remember why but when she called I didn't answer the phone.

She left me three messages.

We were supposed to use the money we'd saved up to buy candy at Costco and then sell it out in front of my house.

I lay under my bed and back then I had pictures of

boys who looked like Jared, my sort of boyfriend from Yellowstone, taped under the bed frame. I had problems.

She called again.

I let it ring.

It stopped and I thought, I am never, ever, ever leaving this bed unless it's to eat or go to the bathroom and they'll write a dramatic novel about me.

One minute later, Joe walked in.

"What are you doing?" He squatted down so he could see my face, but I didn't see his because I was closing my eyes.

"I'm meditating," I said.

He said, "You're a freak show."

I nodded.

Then he said, "Kim is coming to pick you up in five minutes with Trish."

I looked at him. "She called you?"

"Yeah. Why does she have my cell number?"

I stared at his face. She had his number because one time we prank called him from Trish's cell, and Kim acted like she was a girl named Barbara with a deep voice and she wondered if he wanted to hang out and he was like, uh Barbara. Uh. Sure, Barbara. And Kim said, do you care if we kiss a bit.

I had to suck on a pillowcase to keep from laughing and he said, "Uh. I mean. Who is this?"

So that's why she had his cell number.

I told Joe, "Call her back and tell her I'm not going."

"I'm not calling her back," he said.

"Call her, please."

He said. "No." Then he said, "What. Are you two in a fight?" A smile on his fat face.

We were not in a fight.

I was just sad at her.

That was one time and like I said, I don't even remember why.

But after Smiths. After she lied to me, I was more sad than I had ever been in my life.

Ever.

And I would always remember.

Always.

I thought, I will never ever talk to you again, Kim. I won't.

Is that funny? Ahhahahahahahahahahahahahahahahaha.

Because now she's dead and I can't get her to talk to me no matter how hard I try.

• 74 •

I was fifteen minutes late for Dr. Ted's presentation, but it looked like it didn't matter.

Outside Meeting Room A was a huge group of people.

Huge.

The same big blond-haired lady from last year was holding a clipboard and had on headphones and was yelling something that I couldn't hear.

"What's going on?" I asked a man standing next to me.

"He's a no-show," the man said.

"What?"

"He ain't coming," the man said. "The doctor."

A lady in front of me yelled, "I drove here all the way from El Paso!"

The blond woman in charge did a huge whistle and everyone quieted.

"I'm sorry to all of you. I'm sorry for your trouble," she said.

"To hell with our trouble," someone yelled. "Where is he?"

I felt bad for the woman. This was a bad crowd. An angry crowd and I understood why. Dr. Ted Farnsworth made people crazy.

She shouted, "Dr. Farnsworth is feeling sick. He's very sick," she said.

"Bull crap," someone yelled.

"Get him out here. We paid good money!"

I stood.

"I'm so sorry," she said again. "We'll make sure you all get your money back if you'll make an orderly line right here and sign your name and address."

There was more swearing and yelling and the same lady with blue hair was there. She was yelling, too.

Dr. Ted Farnsworth was sick.

He was too sick to help these people cross over the veil.

They all moved to the wall to form an orderly line.

What do I do now?

Some days, actually day number two of avoiding your best friend who keeps texting you and texting you and texting you, on that day, your fake friend named Gabby finds you in the bathroom and asks you what's wrong.

On that day I ignore her and shove my way out the door.

On that day I eat corn dogs across the quad from them.

On that day in the middle of lunch, my best friend falls off her chair onto the cement, and Gabby screams and everyone gets quiet and she says, "Somebody!"

And on that day I take another bite of my corn dog.

Time slows down, a hot-air balloon overhead. The sounds.

I dip the corn dog in ketchup and I take a bite.

I think about that bite every day.

Gabby screaming.

Someone next to me saying, "What's going on?"

People standing up.

And I'm eating.

After I swallow the bite, I look over.

I stand up, too, like everyone else.

Gabby is yelling at me, I think. She's looking over at me and yelling, and I can't understand what she's saying, but I go there. I go over to where Kim is on the concrete.

I get to Kim and her body is on the ground and she is holding her arms to her chest and everything tight, like she has been frozen.

This has happened before. She's passed out before but this one is different. I can feel that this one is different.

Gabby is yelling things like, "Do something. Do something!" And people are standing around and then there is this portal of time when everything stops.

S T O P P E D.

＊ ＊ ＊

One time, I jumped off the Stratosphere. Dad bought us all tickets and Joe said, "Emmy won't do it."

"Yeah, I will," I said.

Joe laughed.

So then I stood on the edge of the platform, and I looked down and my stomach dropped. The itty-bitty pinpoints below, the lights of the city, and I knew the wire was going to break, and I knew they'd have to scrape me off the ground, and I knew that I was wearing bad underwear.

I stood there and there were voices, Joe saying something. My mom telling him to be quiet. The man saying to take my time.

I stood there and I couldn't do it. I knew I couldn't do it.

So I closed my eyes.

I closed my eyes and held my breath, and then I took a step and right when I did it I tried to undo it, I tried to not do it, to turn around and not do it, but it didn't work.

I fell.

And in the middle of the air everything STOPPED.

Everything in front of me, everything behind me, everything everywhere. STOPPED.

And then time came rushing back.

"HELP HER!" Gabby was screaming.

"Kim?"

I knelt down next to her. Touched her arm. "Kim?" I said. "Kim. Look at me. Kim."

She didn't move.

"Kim.

"Breathe.

"Breathe.

"Breathe."

"Is she dead?" Gabby sobbed. "Is she dead?"

I looked up at Gabby. Her and Skeeter and Tony and those idiots. Everyone I knew standing around. Tears were pouring down Gabby's cheeks. And they were all looking at me. I was Kim's best friend.

Me.

I looked back at Kim's face. Tried to focus.

What do I do?

And then it happened. I felt myself say, "Move away."
For the first time in my life, people listened.

I got close to her ear and I whispered, "Come back.
Come back, Kim."

Right then I felt something. I felt something shift. The
world or my body or her body or something between us
shifted.

Right then, her mouth, her slack mouth, her frozen
body moved. Something so small that I was probably
the only one who saw it. Her terrorized body took a
small breath and she whispered to me, "I love you."

I love you.

And then there was the nurse and the paramedics and
teachers and people yelling, and I got shoved back and I
sat there and everything was blurry.

They pumped her chest hard. Pumping pumping.

"Get them out of here," the paramedic yelled. "Clear
out."

Teachers voices in the distance, telling people to go to
class, and I looked over and Gabby stood there.

Everyone moved away but her. She was alone and her arms were to her sides and she was alone. Standing over there.

They were pounding on Kim's chest and the whole world was quiet again.

76

For forty-five minutes, the blond lady took names and address and swearing-people's complaints. She assured the crowd that Dr. Ted Farnsworth would answer all of them himself.

"He will get back to each an every one of ya," she said.

I wanted to say no he won't but instead I stood against the wall and watched.

Waited.

I should've left.

I had two and a half hours until I had to meet Kim, which really wasn't that much time because it took forever to get home, and then I'd have to deal with my mom who was probably freaking out right now, and then I had to get out to Red Rock.

But still I waited.

I had to talk to him.

When the line had cleared out, and the lady started to walk away, I ran to catch her.

"Is he here?" I asked.

She turned and looked at me. Her face was older than it seemed from far away. Deep wrinkles and sagging lips. Lots and lots of makeup. She and Dr. Ted Farnsworth could be twins. Good from far away, old and messy up close.

"I'm sorry, honey. But he's not." She started walking again.

I was right behind her. Her pants so tight you could see the dimples.

"Can I at least talk to him? Just for a second," I said.

She waved her hand at me but didn't stop.

We rounded two corners and she was ignoring me even though there's no way she didn't know I was there.

Finally, I got in front of her and blocked her way. Tony's move.

"Just for a second," I said.

She sighed. "You serious?"

"I'm serious."

She blew out a big burst of air and then looked at her

watch. Then she said, "Look, do yourself a favor and go on home. This is no place for kids. Forget you ever heard of Dr. Ted Farnsworth."

Then she went around me and walked out the emergency exit.

I followed her.

77

The teacher drew a picture of a heart on the board.

It was seventh period and I sat in my desk and sat there.

I am a horrible person.

A horrible horrible person.

I had been ignoring her.

I had been avoiding her.

I had been trying to be nowhere.

Then an aide brought in a piece of paper for Mr. McDog.

McDog stopped talking about integers and studied it for three minutes. Three and a half minutes on the clock, all the while, I thought, I wonder if she's dead.

He cleared his throat. "Today at lunch, one of the students here had a medical issue. Kim Porter?" McDog's voice was nasally and when he said Kim's name it felt weird. Like he shouldn't say her name. He didn't know her.

He wrote the words on the board: CONGENITAL HEART DISEASE, and then he drew a picture of a heart on the board. A really bad picture that he was trying to copy from the handout.

He was not supposed to release medical information. I was going to tell him that and that my dad was going to sue him.

But then I just sat there.

"Here," he said, pointing to a tube. "Here is the problem for Kim."

I stared at the tube. The tube that had wreaked havoc. The tube that caused the puke and the hospital and the surgeries. The tube that was responsible for Dr. Ted Farnsworth and dead websites and books and books and books.

He started saying other things. Shunt. Blood vessels. Pressure and I thought, he has no idea what he's talking about.

"She is going to be okay," Mr. McDog said, "but the principal felt we should all have a rap session about this."

A rap session about heart disease.

Who does that? Who even says that?

"She's going to be okay," McDog said again. "Does anyone have any questions?"

No one raised their hands.

I stared at my fingernails. Kim had helped me paint them green with purple dots for Easter.

Lafe Thompson said, "Is she going to be paralyzed or something?"

I looked up at McDog.

"I just said she's going to be okay, Lafe."

Someone else asked, "Isn't it weird to be fourteen and have heart disease? Like doesn't that mean you're going to die young?"

My heart thumped.

McDog turned red. He read the piece of paper again and then he said, "We're really just supposed to talk about your feelings. How are all of you feeling?"

We sat.

And sat.

And sat.

Someone made a fart noise and then everyone started laughing.

78

The tour bus was in the parking garage again, but this time
it was parked behind some Dumpsters.

I hid beside a Honda as the lady walked up to the bus,
knocked on the door, and went inside.

Five minutes later she came out.

"You can't keep doing this, Gary. You just can't," she said.
Loud.

Gary? Who was Gary?

Someone said something back. She was yelling now, her
voice echoing throughout the parking garage.

"We are running out of money."

A response I couldn't hear.

Then she said, "I'm not doing this anymore. You think that was fun? You think this is funny? Screw you," and then she slammed the door shut.

She walked past me, muttering and swearing, stopped for a second to pick up something off the ground, and then went back into the casino.

I took a breath.

Please. Please. Please. I could do this. I could.

I stood up and made sure I was alone which I was. I could do this. I could do this. Then I walked up to the bus, opened the door, and went inside to talk to Dr. Ted Farnsworth.

Or Gary.

Or whoever he was.

Dr. Ted was sitting there, in his massage chair, a mess of skin and hair and beer cans. A baseball game was blaring on the TV.

"Darla," he said. "Go away."

He hadn't even bothered to look at me.

"I'm not Darla," I said.

He glanced my way. Then looked back at the game.

"Dr. Farnsworth?" I said.

He waved at me. "I'm sick," he said. "Go away."

And he looked sick. He looked like death.

"I'm sorry," I said. "I just wanted to ask you something."

He rubbed his forehead. "You want your money back? You gonna sue me or something? Because I don't have any money. I have no money."

"I don't want your money."

He laughed at that. Like it was funny. Really, really funny. "You don't want my money? Where you from? Mars?"

"No," I said. "I'm from Summerlin."

He looked at me. "Summerlin?"

"Summerlin."

He shrugged. "Never heard of it."

I sat down on the couch. The couch that I had remembered being plush and expensive but now looked threadbare and cheap. Everything looked cheap.

"You told me I could talk to my friend after she died. You told me it would work."

"That's what I tell everyone," he said.

My blood ran cold.

"That's what you tell everyone?"

He started yelling at the TV. "Hit the ball! Hit the ball, you moron!"

The man at bat didn't hit the ball.

"What about those testimonials?" I said.

He glanced at me. "What?"

"All those people said it worked."

He sighed. "People believe it because they want to believe it. Because they're desperate. No one wants to die."

I tried to breathe. I tried to control my breathing.

He picked up another beer and drank some.

"So you lied."

He looked at me. "I lie all the time. Don't you lie? Everyone lies."

I stared at him.

Lied. Lie. Don't I lie? It felt like the walls were caving in.

I did lie.

Lying to my mom. Lying to my dad. Lying to Skeeter. Lying to Kim. Lying to Gabby. Gabby screaming that I lied. Lied. Lied.

I wiped my forehead. "So you're saying that you can't talk to dead people."

"What does it matter?"

I felt tears start to fill my eyes. It was all too much. Everything.

"I've talked to dead people," I said.

He burped. Then he said, "Maybe you have. Maybe you haven't. Maybe you wanted to so much you made it up in your head and thought you did."

Suddenly I felt anger. I felt it bubble up hard and fast.

"No. I didn't make it up in my head," I said, trying to keep my voice steady. I didn't want him to see me cry. "I didn't do that," I said. "I talked to dead people I didn't want to talk to."

He shrugged. "Then I guess you got the gift."

It got quiet except for the noise of the game. The Giants were up by two. It was a rebroadcast. I'd watched this with my dad months before. Nothing here was real.

Then Dr. Ted Farnsworth said something, he said, "You came with that skinny girl. The dark one, right?"

Now the tears were running down my face.

"She didn't make it, did she?"

I didn't say anything but I guess I didn't need to.

He closed his eyes and leaned back in his chair

"You knew she had heart disease," I whispered. "You knew. She trusted you because you knew."

He sighed. "It was a gamble," he said. "If they come in young, odds are it's either the heart or cancer. Cancer is chemo. Your friend had hair so I guessed heart."

Now I was completely empty.

Then he said something. He said, "This life is a hole," he said. "It's so not worth it."

My heart thumped.

This life is a hole. It's so not worth it.

It's so not worth it.

It's so not worth it.

313

It's so not worth it.

Was he right?

Was it a hole?

I thought about Ms. Homeyer and Ed and how they danced and got married and she wore a mermaid dress. I thought about Baylor and the panther doing the robot and how he looked for me, how he thought I was different and how he only died because of an asthma attack. I thought about Kim. Kim who wanted to live and should have lived but then didn't live. Kim who was my best friend and made everything around her better.

Everything.

He was wrong.

He was wrong.

I had seen dead people.

I had talked to them.

And it was worth it.

He was wrong.

I saw him then. A big bag of bones. Scamming people. Sitting in this stupid bus. With nothing. He had nothing.

Just then the door to the bus opened.

It was the man with the flat top and he said, "You still want to go, Gary?"

Dr. Ted sighed. Put down his beer and looked at his watch.

"I guess so," he said. Then he looked at me. "You need a lift somewhere?"

I wiped my eyes. "What?"

He said, "I have an appointment I need to get to," which didn't make sense because he was supposed to be leading a seminar. He kept going. "We can drop you off if you have someplace you want to go."

I nodded. I did need a ride. "Sure," I said. "There is someplace I want to go."

And so then Dr. Ted Farnsworth, or Gary, and his flat-top friend gave me a ride home in his big-faced TALKING BEYOND!! bus.

After school Gabby was waiting for me.

"Did you know?"

I stood in the hall with my backpack. "Know what?"

"That she was sick."

It never occurred to me that Gabby wouldn't know.
That Kim didn't tell her.

I didn't want to deal with it.

I started to walk toward the door. "I think you knew,"
she said, following me.

I kept walking.

"Did you know, Emmy?"

It seemed an impossible question. Kim's heart disease

had been a part of my whole life. Every day. Every hour. Every minute.

I focused on the doors. I just had to get to the doors.

"Did you know?"

I kept walking.

"Emmy! Did you know?" her voice echoed through the hall and I couldn't do it anymore. "Yes. Of course." I turned to face her. "Of course I knew. Why wouldn't I know?" Almost screaming.

"You should have warned me."

She shoved me against the wall so hard it knocked the breath out of me.

"Why didn't she tell me?

"Why didn't you tell me?"

Tears were pouring down her cheeks, and I was trying to breathe and then she was gone, the doors banging against the wall as she left.

The thing is, Kim wasn't usually sick.

She was usually normal and beautiful and fast and funny and no one would know that she was going to die.

That any second her heart could blow up.

317

• 80 •

We pulled up at 4:42 p.m.

The bus was as long as our house.

Mom was on the front porch.

Dad was, too.

Joe.

And Gabby?

"Looks like you have an entourage," Dr. Ted Farnsworth said.

I nodded. "Yeah. I guess."

I walked to the door "Thanks for the ride."

"Don't sue me."

"I might," I said.

"Okay," he said. And that was it.

I got off the bus just in time to see Gabby jog across the street to her house.

Mom rushed over to me. "Where have you been?"

The bus started to pull away and Dad yelled, "Wait! Emmy, what is going on? Why were you on that thing?" and then he was chasing after it and huffing, and Joe started running, too, and what were they going to do? Grab onto the back? James Bond it inside? Beat him up? Get some advice about the afterlife?

"Dad," I yelled, "it's okay."

Mom had her arms around me. "Did he assault you?"

"No, Mom. Ewww. No."

Joe and Dad kept running until they couldn't anymore, both of them bent over in the middle of the street. Dr. Ted Farnsworth's face on the back of the bus got smaller and smaller and smaller and eventually disappeared.

Mom said, "We've been trying to get a hold of you all day. Gabby told me she saw you leave, and I told her you were at the library and then we went to check."

"Who went to check?"

"Me and Gabby."

319

"Gabby?"

"She was worried about you, so she came over."

"Oh," I said.

I took a deep breath.

"We went to check and you weren't at the main library, so then we checked some other places, but we couldn't find you. And your phone was turned off."

Joe and Dad were back now. "What happened? Who was that guy?"

"I don't know," I said. "I met him with Kim once. He's okay."

"He's okay?" Dad said. "He's okay?"

"Calm down," Mom said.

"I will not calm down," Dad said.

Joe said, "Yeah. That was weird. I wouldn't calm down if I were Dad. The guy looked like a total creeper."

"He's not as bad as he looks," I said, which maybe wasn't true.

I glanced at my watch. I had forty-five minutes.

Mom sighed. "Let's get something to eat. It's been a long day."

"I can't," I said.

Mom looked at me.

"I mean, not right now. I have one more place I have to go."

"Hell," Dad said.

"I'm sorry. This is the last time. The very last time. I promise."

"Where do you have to go?" Mom asked.

I looked at Joe. And then I said, "I have to go out to Red Rock."

• 81 •

After Gabby left me in the hall, I sat there.

And sat there.

And sat there.

Someone turned out the lights.

I stood up and walked outside.

Skeeter was sitting on the grass.

At least I thought he was. He was blurry. Maybe I was crying then, too.

He stood up. "Hey."

"Hey."

Then he was saying something to me but I wasn't listening. I was walking.

I think he walked with me.

I think he was with me and we walked the five miles home because the buses were gone.

I think I was sweating and I think he gave me some water.

I think when we got to my house I walked in and I think I left him on our front lawn.

I think I crawled under my bed and I think I cried and cried and cried.

• 82 •

Mom drove me.

I didn't have my stuff.

No Snickers, no Skittles, no *Ladyhawke*.

Mom looked straight ahead and let me sit there.

"Where to?" she said once we'd gotten past the houses and were coming to the turn off.

"Just drop me off at the visitors' center," I said.

She nodded. Then she said, "Can I come with you?"

I looked at her. She was such a good person and I had been so horrible. So horrible. To her. To Gabby. To everyone.

"I have to do this alone but I promise, I promise that I will tell you everything tonight. Everything."

She glanced at me.

"What do you have to do?"

I took a breath. "I don't know," I said. I watched raindrops hit the windshield. "I guess say good-bye?"

She gripped the steering wheel tighter, a tear escaping down her cheek.

"Okay," she finally said, and I said, "Okay." And we drove into the parking lot.

"Should I wait here?"

"No. I'll get home."

"How?"

"I'll walk down to the bus stop."

"Emmy, it's more than five miles."

"I know," I said. "Kim and I used to do it all the time."

She thought about it for a few seconds and I said a prayer, a prayer that she would let me go. That one more time, just one more time, she'd let me go.

"Do you have your cell phone?"

I pulled it out to show her.

"Call me when you're done," she said. "I'll be waiting at home. We all will be."

My heart thumped. They'd all be waiting for me.

"Okay."

The clock said 5:22.

I opened the door to get out and she said, "Emmy?"

I looked at her. "What?"

"I'm here for you."

I nodded. "I know."

She smiled.

I closed the door and watched her drive away.

And then I was alone in the rain.

• 83 •

I went to the hospital with Mom the day after Kim collapsed.

I even put on lipstick. I don't know why.

Kim was in the usual unit on her usual floor.

She was not doing well. Mom had been on her cell with Trish and Kim was not doing well at all, Mom said.

"Oh," I said.

Mom looked at me when I said that, "It's worse than usual," she said in the elevator.

"I heard," I said. Then I looked at a poster on the wall of a bunch of babies.

She was not doing well but it would be okay. This had

happened a few times before and it always worked out. It took time, but eventually she'd be okay.

She'd be okay.

We got off the elevator and Mom walked quickly.

I walked behind her.

And I didn't want to be there. I wanted to be anywhere else. Anywhere but there.

I knew all I'd have to do was sit. Watch bad movies or play Uno with Kim or, if she was too tired, with Mom or Trish.

I'd eat chips from the vending machines and do MASH over and over and over again until Kim and I got the boys we wanted.

It wasn't hard to be the friend. You didn't have to have the tubes and the medicine and the shots and the doctors.

But that day was a tunnel. A dark black tunnel.

Trish was out in the nurses' area talking to a lady.

Mom said she was going to help her. "You check on Kimmer," she said.

I nodded. "Okay."

Mom hurried over.

I stood.

And then I moved.

Barely.

I stopped just outside Kim's door and stared at her name on the whiteboard.

Kim Porter. Someone had made the "o" in her name a heart. I almost erased it with my finger but then I didn't.

This is nothing.

Everything will be fine.

I took a breath and walked into her room.

It was worse than I'd ever imagined.

Things beeping, her skin white-leather, the smell heavy and sterile. I had to stop myself from reacting. I'd never seen her like that. Ever.

She opened her eyes.

"Hey," she said. Her voice soft.

"Hey."

She struggled to sit up.

"Don't worry," I said. "You don't have to worry. Just lie there."

She said, "I'm okay."

I said, "Yeah. I know."

She nodded. Then she said, "Your lips look pretty."

I touched my mouth. I didn't think she'd notice. I don't know why, she was the one person who always noticed.

I sat down next to her. "I was just playing around," I said.

"I like it," she said.

"You do?"

"Yeah."

She closed her eyes for a second and I watched her chest. I watched it go up and down and up and down. She was going to be fine. She was always fine.

"So," she said, her eyes still closed. "Are you mad at me?"

I swallowed. "What?"

"You're mad at me, right?"

"No."

"You're not?"

I tried to think what to say. I *was* mad at her. I was really really mad at her.

"I don't know," I said.

It was all so stupid. She could make other friends. She could go to parties and wear tight clothes. She could have boys pick her up at the grocery store. She could do whatever she wanted.

"What did I do?" she said.

I twisted my ring on my finger. I just wanted things to go back to normal.

I started to say something when Mom walked in. "Hey, Missy." She walked over and stroked Kim's hair. "How're you feeling?"

"Not too good," Kim said.

Mom reached for her water and helped her drink some. "You'll be okay. We just need to get you strong again. Your mom is talking to your doctors."

Kim nodded.

I stood there.

Mom looked at me. She could tell something was wrong. But she didn't ask. Instead she straightened Kim's pillow and sat down.

"You want to watch something?"

Kim looked at me. I shrugged.

"Yeah," she said. "Sure."

I sat down on a couch across the room.

Mom turned on the TV and *1000 Ways to Die* was on. Mom started to switch it and Kim said, "Let's watch this."

Mom looked at her and I tried not to laugh. No way my mom was going to let us watch this show. Kim knew it. "You want to watch this?" Mom said.

"It's very intellectual," Kim said. "I think it will make me feel better."

Mom looked at me.

"It is quite intellectual," I said.

"And addicting." Kim smiled. "You should ask Joe."

So for the next three hours, we watched reruns of *1000 Ways to Die*. Trish came in and didn't say a word. Just sat down.

We watched someone die from eating too much ketchup, someone die sledding down a mountain of pancakes, someone die from the static of a microphone.

Mom kept going, "Girls, let's change it." Or "Oh my, is this true?" Or "What did he just say?"

Trish said, "Linda, you're getting into this," and Mom blushed. "No I'm not."

We were laughing so hard. At least I was. Kim was sort of laughing but you could tell it hurt.

But still. She was laughing.

Maybe everything was going to be okay.

• 84 •

Dr. Farnsworth, Gary, advocated nature. Visitations could happen anywhere but getting back to God's creations made crossing the veil that much simpler.

So we picked a trail that was pretty easy to hike and every time we'd been there, there were other people. Tourists or locals or climbers or bikers.

Today, with the rain, there was no one in sight.

I started up the trail. She died in eight minutes. Eight minutes. If I went hard, I could make it.

As I began to hike, the rain started to pound down.

I took deep breaths and tried to focus.

I will see you.

I can see you.

You will be there.

I didn't bring your treats.

I didn't bring your movie.

I didn't bring your book.

But I brought me.

Just me.

I miss you. You are my best friend.

As I came around the corner to where our rock was in view, I froze.

There was a figure.

Someone.

She stood up when she saw me.

She waved.

My heart pumped and I waved back. I waved back and then I started walking toward her. Faster. And faster.

Soon I was running.

It was happening. This was happening. After everything else, it was finally happening.

• 85 •

If you know someone is going to die for years, for every day of every week, of every month, of every year, sometimes you don't think it's really going to happen.

Even if that person gets close now and then.

She may even be in the hospital and she may look really sick and the nurses may whisper in the hallways but even with all that, she won't die.

She never dies.

* * *

She never ever ever dies.

Until one day, she does.

After a long time sitting and watching TV at the hospital, Kim got a visitor.

It was Gabby.

She stood in the doorway. Her face pale and she was trembling, holding a mug with candy in it.

I looked at my hands.

Trish was in the corner asleep.

Mom saw her. "Oh my goodness, Gabby. Come in."

Gabby didn't move.

Kim saw her for the first time. "Oh hey. Yeah. Come in."

Gabby said, "Okay."

And she sat on the edge of the couch by me.

"How are you?" she said to Kim.

"I'm good."

"Good," she said. "Good."

Kim said, "Yeah."

Then Gabby handed her the cup of chocolate, which was a stupid gift.

I sat there and watched.

"I'm sorry you're sick," Gabby said.

Kim shrugged and smiled. "It's okay."

Gabby nodded. Then she said, "I'm glad you didn't die."

Just like that, I'm glad you didn't die.

Kim laughed. "I'm never going to die, right, Ems?"

I felt like I couldn't breathe. Like I was being strangled.

"Ems?" Kim said. Gabby looked at me and I knew any minute, any second, I was going to burst.

I stood up. "I'll be right back."

"Where are you going?"

I shook my head. Mom looked at me. "Are you okay?"

I nodded. "I just need some air."

Mom said something else. Or maybe it was Kim.

Or maybe even Gabby.

I don't know because as soon as I was out of that room I started running.

I ran.

And ran

And ran.

I didn't stop until I was down the stairs, through the lobby, and out into the heat.

And there, right there in front of the roundabout and the taxis and the people in wheelchairs, right there I sank to the cement and started to bawl.

Kim died three minutes after I left.

Kim died without me.

I let her die without me.

• 87 •

I got closer and the figure got bigger and then I slowed.

It wasn't Kim.

It wasn't Kim at all.

It was Skeeter.

* * *

I stopped in the middle of the trail.

"Hey," he yelled.

I didn't move.

"Emmy?"

It was Skeeter.

I didn't understand.

But part of me felt relieved.

Why did I feel relieved?

I had let my best friend down and I was doing it again.

But then he was coming toward me. I kept walking.

Dear Kim. What does this mean? Where are you? Why aren't you here?

And then he was standing in front of me.

"Hey."

"Hey."

"I've been waiting for you."

The rain still going and we were both soaked. He was wearing a Descendants T-shirt, his headphones around his neck, and he was carrying a plastic bag.

"I brought us food."

"You brought us food?"

"Yeah," he said. "But it's mostly gone." He held it out for me to see and it was full of wrappers.

"How long have you been here?"

He wiped his face but it didn't do much good, the water was running down.

"I've been here since eight."

"Eight?"

"Eight."

"Eight in the morning?"

"Eight in the morning."

My heart was thumping and I didn't even know why.

"Why?"

He shook his head. Looked at his feet and then shook his head again. Then he said, "I knew you'd come. I knew you'd be here sometime. I didn't . . . I didn't want to, you know, miss you."

I took a breath. He didn't want to miss me.

"You've been waiting for me all day?"

He looked at me. "I guess I have."

"Why?"

"Why?"

"Yeah. Why?"

"Because."

Because . . .

* * *

"Because." He stopped and I waited. I waited and he said,
"Because."

And then he took my face in his hands.

And I almost died. I almost died right then.

He took my face in his hands and he did what I never thought
would ever happen to me. Ever. In a million years.

He took my face in to his hands, the water pouring down,
and he kissed me.

· 88 ·

When it was over and I was shaking, he said, "I'm sorry."

And I laughed. "You don't have to say sorry."

I looked at my watch. 5:48. On the dot.

I looked up at the sky.

He looked with me.

We stood there. For a minute. For more than a minute, and for the first time, in a long time, I felt free. I felt happy. I felt alive.

I knew she knew. I knew it. And she was happy, too.

"I think it's going to be okay," I said.

He nodded. "I think so, too."

We walked down the two-lane highway toward town.

Barefoot.

And holding hands.

My whole body felt like it was on fire. I had never held hands with a boy before.

I had never seen ghosts before.

I'd never said good-bye to my friend before.

"So," he said, "I looked up Saltair."

I smiled. "I did, too."

"Did you see they play shows there now?"

"No," I said. "I didn't see that."

"Yeah," he said. "They had Paramore last week. And Fun is playing in August."

I started laughing. "Fun? Are you serious?"

"What?"

"Nothing," I said. I couldn't explain.

Then he said, "I thought we could take a road trip one day. Go see a show."

It sounded so perfect. So real. So not me. And of course my mom would never let me go on a road trip with a boy, but I didn't say that. Instead I said, "Yes. We should."

And he smiled.

I smiled too.

And that was it.

• ACKNOWLEDGMENTS •

This novel happened with the help and support of many people:

My agent, Edward Necarsulmer IV, for his enthusiasm and grace.

My editor, Nancy Conescu, for her patience and compassion for pretend people.

My father, Larry Vinson Knight, for always believing in me.

My family, all of them. Who took care of my babies and me while I worked to finish this book.

My readers, Dan Knight, Larry Knight, Katy Knight, Holly Wever, Ally Condie, Kathy Knudsen, Millie Soelberg, Megan Castagnetto, Shelby Russell, Jen White, Janessa Ransom, Carol Lynch Williams, Cheri Earl, Ann Cannon, Heather Dixon, Shar Peterson, Chris Crowe, and more for being willing to read bad bad drafts of a crazytown story.

My sweet husband, Mr. Cameron, who is always there for me.

And of course, Ms. Homeyer. RIP.

Author Q&A—Ann Dee Ellis
The End or Something Like That

What inspired you to write *The End or Something Like That*?

Parts of this story have been rattling around for years. Ms. Homeyer is based off a teacher I had in middle school who actually did pass away in the middle of my eighth-grade year. A friend and I went to her funeral on a whim. When we got there, we were shocked. The church was empty—maybe there were four or five people in the pews. I just assumed that funerals were always packed with people. I've thought about that moment ever since and knew I'd one day write about it.

Did you always know you wanted to be a writer?

I have always loved both reading and telling stories. From a young age, I knew I wanted to be a writer. However, according to a survey I filled out in sixth grade, my ambitions changed—I wanted to be a Solid Gold Dancer, an armpit smeller (that's a real job, P.S. and rumor has it they make a lot of money), or a lawyer. It wasn't until college that I came back to my first love and realized that writing was what I wanted to do (though armpits are still quite appealing).

Did you form any of your characters around yourself or other people you know in real life?

There are snippets of me in almost all the characters I write. And there are snippets of people I know. In *The End*, Kim is based on my true-life best friend from childhood. She and I met in first grade and have been best friends ever since. She is one of the kindest, most beautiful, happiest, craziest people I know. I can't even begin to tell all the misadventures we had together. Like Emmy, I tend to be more cautious and insecure. My friend Kim, on the other hand, is never afraid of anyone or anything. Though the characters in the book are different from both of us, the core of the novel is based on that friendship. Kim and I are still close friends though we live on opposite ends of the country. We use Instagram to check in on each other.

Similarly, did you base any of what happens in the story on real experiences?
The funeral experience was real (though the details were much much different). Also, Kim and I always had conversations about what we would be willing to do for a million dollars (I would wear the same pair of pants for a year; I would go down a waterslide every day, eight hours a day again for a year; I would eat Taco Bell for three meals a day for a year; etc.). And one time I stood on one side of the park and watched while Kim met a boy in the middle of the field and kissed him. I was jealous. I'll admit.

What were some of your favorite books as a child, and how do you think they affect how and what you write today?
My mom was an elementary school librarian. From the time we were small, she would pull my sister and me onto her undulating waterbed, and we'd read book after book each night. I grew up with *Drummer Hoff*, *Corduroy*, *Madeline*, *Petunia*, and others. Later, we moved on to Laura Ingalls Wilder, *The Secret Garden*, *Anne of Green Gables*, etc.

On my own I read whatever I could find but eventually settled on realistic fiction. I loved reading about real people in real life dealing with hard things. Like Ramona cracking a raw egg on her head at lunch. That's just the kind of thing that would happen to me. And in Louise Plummer's book *The Romantic Obsessions* and *Humiliations of Annie Sehlmeier*, the main character got caught toilet papering her crush's car. I read that chapter in the basement of our house and started bawling. My mom happened to come down right then to tell me it was time for lunch. I told her I had NO TIME TO EAT, tears streaming down my face. She asked me what was wrong. I held up the book. She smiled and left me to my grief. I loved *Jane Eyre* and was devastated by *Tess of the D'urbervilles*.

And now, as a reader, I still seek out contemporary realistic fiction. It's my genre. And it's also what I like to write. Stories about real, flawed, strange, brave, but also not-brave people dealing with the things life brings them.

Was it difficult to write alternating plotlines? How did you go about mapping them out?
I am a messy messy writer. I don't outline. I don't write paragraphs. I don't plan. And I never ever write in a straight line. I start out with a character and see what happens.

The real sifting and making sense of things happens in revision. That's when I have to go back and try to figure out what's really going on in the story. I once made a goal to write a book in chronological order, with paragraphs and a clear direction.

It didn't work out.

My poor editor.

What do you hope your readers take away from this story?
I just hope they like it.

Death and loss are tough issues to write about. Did you come across any stumbling blocks while writing? Did the writing process affect you emotionally?
My book launch happened on the one-year anniversary of my mom's death. I didn't realize, until that very day, that this book was maybe my way of saying good-bye. She had a terminal illness for many years, so the process was drawn out and difficult. I really didn't correlate my own situation and Emmy's during the writing process—which seems so obvious now. We all have to deal with death, and we all have different ways of doing that. For me, this book helped me process things I didn't realize I needed to process.

You somehow were able to infuse humor into a book about a pretty serious topic—no easy feat! And yet you do it seamlessly and tastefully. Can you describe how you were able to keep a sense of humor while writing about a subject that's uncomfortable for many people?
First off it's important to understand that I'm kind of weird. And I think bizarre things. And I do odd things (ask my sister—she would get so annoyed with me growing up). And I love to laugh. I can't imagine writing without laughing.

All my books have dealt with heavy themes, but to me they're not so much about topics, but rather about people. Imperfect, happy, sad, confused, strange, normal, not-normal people. People who sit in the closet and eavesdrop. Or ride around on bikes yelling at cars. Or tape stuffed animals to light posts. People who love and want to be loved—despite their weaknesses and imperfections.

Questions for Discussion

1. Using alternating chapters, the author describes two separate experiences from Emmy's perspective, one beginning with Ms. Homeyer's funeral and one documenting Emmy's friendship with Kim and how she copes with Kim's subsequent death. How are the two stories really like one story? What similarities do they share, and how are they different?

2. What do you think about Trish's decision to go against Kim's wishes by having her cremated and arranging a funeral that "Kim would have hated"? Do you think it speaks to Kim's relationship with her mother? Does it have more to do with Kim's age? Or is it something else? Explain.

3. Do you think Kim truly believed in the idea of communicating with the dead? Why or why not?

4. On page 48 Emmy says, "People used to talk about me and Kim. They never fight. They never disagree. They never get jealous. It's like they were made for each other." Do you agree that Emmy and Kim were meant to be friends? Discuss their friendship and why you felt it was a perfect match, or not.

5. Las Vegas, Nevada, is the backdrop for Emmy's story. Given what you know about the city, explain how it brings out the themes of the novel.

6. While Kim accepts death as an inevitability and often makes light of it, Emmy denies it and is uncomfortable when Kim discusses it openly. Consider both Kim and Emmy's characters and compare their approaches to dealing with death. What does each approach say about their individual characters?

7. Throughout the text, Emmy is doubtful about the possibility of communicating with Kim after her death, yet she's also desperate to succeed at it when the time comes. Why do you think that is?

8. What do you think it means that Emmy sees other dead people like Ms. Homeyer, Baylor Frederick Hicks, and Kim's uncle Sid, but never Kim herself?

9. Dr. Ted Farnsworth appears in the text at two integral moments in the plot, and his philosophies are mentioned over the course of the novel. How does his character affect Emmy's journey to find reconciliation with the pain she's dealing with?

10. When Emmy goes up to Red Rock for the last time, she is surprised to see Skeeter there instead of Kim's ghost. Describe how seeing Skeeter is an important part of Emmy's evolution as a character.